MERCE

J.P. Hart

DEDICATION

To all of the people who encouraged me, inspired me, and stuck by me every step of the way. You are the reason MERCE is real and I thank you from the bottom of my heart and soul.

To all of the people who said I couldn't do it.
flips the bird Believe me now, bitches?

CONTENTS

J.P. Hart

ACKNOWLEDGMENTS

First and foremost, I have to acknowledge and thank my beloved Huz Beast. Honey, you are the best Beastie in existence. You are my everything. Thank you for making the coffee and fielding the questions and requests that would have drawn me back into reality. Thank you for your endless dedication to Call of Duty and Borderlands while I was writing. And most of all, thank you for being the front line against my own stupidity. You smell funny and your face is annoying.

Secondly, I need to thank my family, both chosen and blood, for inspiriting so many…umm…unique characters. Without you, I would have nothing to write about.

And of course, my Reader Minions and Opinion Drones. Thank you for putting up with my constant PSSSST… HEY! HEYYYYYY! M'ere. I need your opinion on something:

Tera Fritze (for being my first addict)

Erica Would (for adding fuel to that fire)

Nick King (for CONSTANTLY reminding me that only I could kill my dream)

Denny Baker (for pointing out my grammatical mistakes in the first draft… on Facebook)

Scotty Bowden (for loving my book, regardless of the quality, because you love me)

Lameh Cortes (for just plain getting it and being excited to read my book, even though you're not a nerd)

Kate Voorheis (for very promptly hounding me for more pages)

And finally, you, the reader.

Without you, all of this would just be word vomit on a page and a waste of time.

Chapter 1

"Your trial starts tomorrow," the doctor said, looking at Jessie from over the rim of her designer glasses. The woman was kind enough as far as Jessie could tell. But, like 99% of the "medical professionals" she'd encountered in her lifetime of head shrinking experts, her ultimate goal was to be that lime-light author of the next get-to-know-the-monster memoir.

"Good," Jessie said calmly as she looked everywhere but at the doctor. She'd been in the prison's interview room about a hundred times at that point. She'd long since memorized every crack in the blue painted concrete walls. There were new scratches in the steel table, though. She ran her fingers over them lazily. Normally she needed skin to skin contact to feel other people's emotions. But, if she concentrated hard enough she could feel the frustration and rage of the person who'd slammed their cuffed wrists into the table. Apparently, their plea deal had fallen through. "Maybe they'll give me the death penalty so I can finally get some goddamned sleep."

"You want to be found guilty?" the doctor asked. Jessie waited as the silver click pen she was constantly fidgeting with went flying across her notepad. It was yellow that day, and longer than the usual. She'd come prepared, really hoping to get some good material for her book.

"Not really," Jessie admitted. "But, what are the chances of them letting me out?" she asked once the doctor looked up again. "As far as the people in this town are concerned, I killed thirty people in just under an hour."

"It depends. Do you believe you killed them?" the doctor asked, scribbling away.

That was the million dollar question.

"No," she said and the doctor started writing again. "Yes," she said while the doctor's head was still down and the pen was scratching away. "Final answer?" she asked as the doctor looked up in confusion. "I don't know. Can I phone a friend?" she asked much to the doctor's irritation.

"I really wish you would take this more seriously," the doctor said. "I'm just trying to help you."

Jessie sighed as she looked to the dingy window and started to chew on her thumbnail. She wanted to explain what had happened, but she didn't know how without it making her sound crazy. *Tell her the* truth, the reasonable voice whispered. *If they understand, they can help us.* It seemed logical enough. That's what medical professionals were for, right?

Tell them the truth so they can chop us up into little pieces, the malignant voice whispered with a cackle. *Wouldn't that be fun? Snipandcutandsnipandcutandsnipandcut. Let's see what our insides look like.*

"Shut up," Jessie whispered and put her hands over her ears to block them out, but she knew it wouldn't work. They were in her head. "Damn it."

"Jessie?" the doctor asked carefully. "Are you alright?"

"What do you think?" she asked with a growl. The endless chatter inside her brain, clawing at the back of her eyes, was making her feel like an exposed nerve. "You try living with the screams ricocheting constantly in your skull," she said, hitting the side if her head. "Then, tell me that you're alright."

"Is the medication helping at all?" the doctor asked as Jessie centered herself in her chair and straightened her spine. *In, one, two, three, out, one, two, three, repeat* the reasonable voice chanted in a soothing tone, trying to calm her from the inside out as the malignant voice began to sing "They're Coming to Take Me Away, Ha-Haaa!" at increasing volume.

"Sometimes," Jessie answered through gritted teeth.

"But, not now."

"I just took it before they brought me in here," she explained. "Give it a few minutes and they'll calm down."

They sat in silence as Jessie began building a mental wall between her and the voices. She concentrated on soundproofing the shit out of the inside until she could barely hear the malignant voice screaming in frustration. It didn't like being ignored.

When the din had calmed to a dull roar and Jessie was able to think again, she waved her hand for the doctor to continue.

"Can I ask you about what happened that day without it triggering an episode?" the doctor asked.

"You should," she said, but she had to fight an involuntary twitch as the walls she'd constructed started to crack.

"How do you remember it happening?" the doctor asked. Jessie breathed deeply through her nose and exhaled through her mouth. Her heartbeat was climbing and a cold sweat was creeping steadily across her scalp. She ran her hand under her mile long braid and it came away clammy. "Tell me, from your perspective," the doctor said with a slow wave of her hand.

It started with a whisper, the reasonable voice in Jessie's head prompted her as it carried through the spreading cracks. It had been pushing her to tell them the full truth, but her logic failed to see the benefit of full disclosure.

"It started with a whisper," Jessie said out loud before the voice had finished its sentence, unable to resist its urging. Her eyes tracked the dust motes in the room, floating quietly with them as she tried to get out of her own head. "Is the heater on?" she asked suddenly, trying to distract the doctor from her line of questioning. She'd been willing to answer at first, but the thought of a full blown incident scared her too much.

"No," the doctor said, but it sounded more like a question than a statement. *She's afraid of you. You need to keep calm.*

"It's burning up in here," Jessie told her. Fear crept quietly into her skin, making her flesh crawl. Her medication was different that day. She'd never taken it before, but the stress of the trial was making her episodes more frequent and violent. She'd been too desperate for relief to question it. She wished then that she had. What if the new medicine didn't work as well? What if she lost control?

Alarm registered briefly in the doctor's eyes before she stood from her blue plastic chair. She raised her hand to the AC vent set into the concrete in the corner of the room and shook her head.

"It's blowing ice cold," she said turning back to the table and pulling a pen light out of the breast pocket of her white coat. Jessie jerked back with a hiss as she reached for the side of her face and clicked the light on.

"Don't," she said, sharper than she meant to. "The medicine is giving me a headache," she said as the doctor looked at her in growing concern. "Honest," she lied. She was already on edge, feeling whatever emotions were running through the doctor might just be the push she needed. "Check my chart. They gave me something new today. It's probably just the adjustment."

"Your chart says they gave you Thorazine," the doctor said, but Jessie knew it had been different. She knew what her Thorazine looked like. It was a relief every time she saw the little orange pill. The one they gave her before her appointment was white.

"Huh," Jessie said with a shrug, trying to play it off like it was no big deal. "I must not have been paying attention. Maybe it's just the fact that I haven't gotten much sleep."

"Is it the angel?" the doctor asked. "Or the demon?"

Jessie momentarily regretted calling them that. She'd only referred to the voices that way to help the doctor put it in perspective, not because she truly believed she had an angel and a demon in her head.

"Neither," she said. It wasn't a complete lie. "I keep hearing them screaming. I can't shut them out."

"The people who died in the community center?" the doctor asked, going back to her seat and starting up with the scribbling again. Jessie lifted her head slightly to try and read what the doctor was writing without taking the notepad away. The words "possible breakthrough" headed the page.

"Regret does strange things to people," Jessie said absently. *Tell her you can't believe you did it.* "I just don't understand how I could have done it. I don't even remember going inside."

"You never did," the doctor said, focusing on Jessie hard enough to make her flinch. "They recovered the security footage from the convenience store across the street. You stood at the edge of the property and just stared at the outside until the fire started."

"I still feel guilty, though," Jessie said, fighting with the frustration brewing just under the surface. Why was it so hard to understand? "I should have done something to stop it."

Nausea clawed at Jessie's stomach at the memory of watching the carnage unfold within the walls of the community center the day she was arrested. She didn't have to be inside physically to remember what happened to the people trapped inside. The voices showed it all to her, playing the mental snuff film in real time in a stunning, high definition broadcast directly into frontal lobe. *Presented in Technicolor and Sponsored by Pepsi.*

Jessie swallowed the chunks rising in her throat and ignored the sickness as best she could.

The doctor sat in silence as she studied Jessie. She knew what the doctor was thinking. Humans were hard wired to protect their kind when they knew it was within their power to do so. Heroes acted on that impulse, even if it meant sacrificing themselves in the process. Cowards hid. Villains watched believing that what they did, they did for the greater good. Evil just didn't care.

"Do you believe that you could have saved them?"

"I know I could," Jessie said.

"Then, why didn't you?"

Jessie breathed through her nose and out through her mouth, closing her eyes and counting to ten to try and slow her heart rate. "Because," she said with a careless shrug. "At the time, I just didn't care."

"Because of Daniel?" the doctor asked.

Jessie twitched as the image of her nephew slammed hard into her frontal lobe. The sun was warm that day. It was July. Independence Day. "They took him," she said through gritted teeth. He was wearing his favorite shirt. It was white, with a picture of a frowning T-Rex. "If you're happy and you know it clap your," she sang softly, remembering the words on his shirt. "They took him from me," she said, staring at the doctor.

"There's no evidence that the men from the community center abducted your nephew," the doctor said.

"They did it," she said with a hiss. She knew they did it. She'd hunted them. Hunted them down to the place where they stashed Daniel. He was gone. *Not a trace.* But, she knew it was them. She could still smell them in the air. They laughed at him. They called him demon spawn. "The old man will pay that much?"

"Pay for what, Jessie?" the doctor asked.

"That's what they asked," she whispered. They'd been watching Daniel with her in the park that day. They were playing hide and seek. He was hiding. *Seekseekseek. Oh boy did we seekseekseek. We killed them. They took him.*

"There was no evidence of foul play in Daniel's disappearance, Jessica," the doctor said.

Jessie slammed her hand on the table, causing the legs to groan in protest under the impact. "I found all your God damned evidence," she said in a low growl. "I found enough to hang them all, but you all ignored it. You said I made it up. You tried to accuse me of killing him, but you couldn't pin it on me, so you let me go."

"The 'evidence' you found was nothing more than a torn child's shirt and a beer bottle. You couldn't even show the authorities where to find the barn where you claimed you found it," the doctor said calmly, but the fear in her eyes betrayed her. She was terrified.

"All you had to do was feel it," Jessie said. The reasonable voice was screaming at her to calm the fuck down, but the malignant voice was pissed. They all loved Daniel like he was theirs. It was the one thing they could agree on. "If you had felt it, you would have seen what I saw. You would have felt it. You would have understood. They deserved to die."

"I'm going to call the guard," the doctor said.

All three voices snapped to attention at once; Jessie, the reasonable, and the malignant. They couldn't afford an incident the night before her trial. Without thinking, Jessie slipped into the doctor's mind. She ferreted out the fear of Jessie, chased it into the open, and squashed it.

The doctor's face went blank and serene. Jessie removed the last few minutes. The doctor knew she was crazy. She didn't need the mental proof. When she'd rewound the doctor's memories to just before she'd mentioned Daniel, Jessie breathed deep and let her mind go.

"I'm tired, doc," she said. "Can I go back to my cell?"

"Sure," the doctor said with a hint of disappointment. She didn't get everything she'd hope for in the way of material. She'd just have to make do with her notes.

Chapter 2

Jessie stretched her neck from side to side and rolled her head forward on her shoulders in front of the squat mirror in the courthouse waiting room. She was trying to stretch the fabric of the demure blouse her attorney, Zack, had picked out for her. She felt like an imposter in the drab, yet somehow feminine pantsuit. The dark circles hanging under her eyes were the only part of her she recognized in her reflection. Zack had been insistent that she play down her more unnerving and "exotic" physical qualities. He said it was to make her more appealing to the conservative, morally outraged citizens of the jury.

"Here," he said, handing her a small pot of concealer that matched her porcelain skin tone. "For the bags under your eyes," he said in explanation to her unspoken question. "You look like shit, kid."

"Don't call me kid," she said. "I'm 22 not 12."

After her session with the good doctor, she'd been escorted back to her cell in solitary confinement without incident. As a reward for her behavior, the night guard had given her a set of clear plastic headphones and a clear plastic radio for her to listen to. The guard wasn't a bad lady, despite her butch hair-cut and sour expression. She even seemed to understand the effect the music had on Jessie. Most people frowned at the fact that the only thing that seemed to bring her some semblance of peace was the violent rhythm and angry guitar riffs of metal.

"How did you sleep?" Zack asked behind her as she used her

finger to smear the concealer under her mismatched eyes like war paint. She looked at his reflection and raised an eyebrow, waiting for him to look up from the file folder holding his case notes. He was a plain man with neat, brown hair and watery blue eyes. He was barely 5'10" in his loafers and was bureaucrat thin, but compared to her he was a giant. She guessed it was just the intellectual bad-ass in him that made him seem bigger than he really was. Then again, she was only 5'1" barefoot. Feeling small was normal.

When he lifted his eyes to meet her pale blue and green stare, he seemed confused. "What?"

"I'm standing trial for thirty counts of murder and arson," she pointed out. "How do you think I slept?"

"With the litany of medications and tranquilizers they keep you on in the prison, I would think you'd have been comatose," he said with a disappointed shake of his head. "I still don't like the fact that they keep making you take that stuff."

"They're just trying to help," she reminded him. "Speaking of," she said as a thought occurred to her. "Dr. Faustus said they gave me my Thorazine yesterday, but the pill they gave me was white. Do you know anything about that?"

"The prison psychologist's name is Dr. Nguyen," he said first. "And no. They weren't supposed to change your medication, as much as I hate how dull they make you. Did it at least help you sleep?"

She shrugged. "I did get a little rest. Olga gave me back my music when it got too loud."

"Her name's Geraldine," her attorney corrected her. Again.

Jessie shrugged. "She looks more like an Olga to me."

"How's the noise now?" he asked.

"It's there," she said. She bit her lip in concern. After almost losing her shit with the doctor, she'd tongued her meds that morning when she saw they were white. "What if I can't keep it together?"

"Dragonforce," he said as he pulled a tiny, square MP3 player from his pocket. A small nub stuck out of the port where the headphones were normally attached, making her frown. "I also threw some Motorhead, Blind Guardian, Ozzy, and a few other things on there for you. It should help keep you level during the trial."

Seeing that she was still afraid, he sighed and put his hand on her shoulder.

"Before you went on the meds, you had to deal with the voices, but you were the one in control of your emotions, yeah? You raised Daniel, happily and without incident until a year ago," he said, making her grit her teeth and look away. "And, that wasn't your fault," he said as he hooked his finger under her chin and made her look him in the eyes. "You didn't physically harm any of those people, Jessie. You stood there and watched the building for almost an hour. No one went in or came out. And, to top it off, it was supposed to be closed that day. The only thing the prosecution has is the fear mongering this town has been slinging your way since you were a kid, but that isn't evidence."

He handed her the MP3 player and waited for her to put it in her pocket before giving her the flesh-toned earbud he'd had made for her. It had a slim profile and looked more like a hearing aid than a headphone, but it was a lifeline under stress.

"Just make sure you keep the volume low and pause it when you don't need it," he said, tucking a few strands of her deep black hair behind her ear. He told her to wear it down for the trial, even though it being in her face drove her nuts. He said it made her sharp features look less severe.

"Thanks, Zack," she said, genuinely relieved. He may not have understood the way Olga did, but he didn't question her preferred brand of tranquilizer. Before the pills, and before Daniel, getting lost in her music was the only relief she had.

"Don't mention it." He smiled down at her sadly. "In fact, just let me do the talking."

"Do you really think they'll let me out?" she asked as he went back to shuffling through his files.

"Honestly?"

"No, Zack, lie to me," she said with an eyebrow raised and her full lips slightly pursed.

"I've travelled all over the country consulting on cases and acting as council for years. I've never once taken a case I wasn't 100% sure I could win, especially pro bono," he reminded her. "But, the witch hunt this town has launched against you for the last year does not give me the warm and fuzzies. My biggest fear in this case is that the jury isn't going to put aside their prejudices."

Jessie felt like she'd been punched in the chest. It was bad enough her family couldn't handle her being around anymore after what happened to her nephew. If she did get out of prison, she'd have nowhere to go. "Maybe it would be better for them to give me the death penalty," she said quietly.

"Don't say that, kiddo," he said, putting his files down and coming back to gather her into a strong hug. "We'll figure this out. I promise."

She hugged him back limply, trying not to lock up at the embrace. His worry and doubt flooded through her at his touch, making her feel weak in the knees until he released her. As soon as she was free, she reached into her pocket and hit the play button on the MP3 player to try and block out his emotions and memories.

"Who's Bernal?" she asked after a minute of focusing on the beat of *Through the Fire and Flames*. An image swam up from the murky echoes of her attorney's memories of an older man, half bent from age until he was just above her height with a face like worn leather and a scalp of thick hair that was more grey than black.

His eyes snapped to hers in shock as soon as the question left her lips. "It's creepy when you do that," he said after a pause. "He's an old friend of mine. He called me last night to talk about your case."

"What happened to attorney-client confidentiality?"

Before he could answer her, a sharp knock on the door brought their attention around. A large black man in uniform poked his head in without waiting for an invitation. He wouldn't look at her directly. Then again, no one in town did.

"They're ready for you," he said and ducked back out without another word.

"Showtime," Zack said giving her a reassuring smile.

"Hallelujah," she said in a deadpan tone and followed her attorney through the door.

Camera flashes went off like strobe lights as they walked through the hall to the courtroom. Reporters shouted incoherent questions over the enraged taunts of the protesters lining the walls. In a big city, they would have been forced to wait on the steps to keep some form of peace and professionalism in the courthouse. But, in the backwater town of Rankine, TX, there weren't enough police officers to keep them out.

"Burn in Hell," a woman shouted as she threw a chunk of brick she'd smuggled in under her coat.

The projectile missed Jessie's head narrowly, making her pause mid-step and turn. The heat crept back into Jessie's skin, uninhibited by the medication, as malice slipped around her like a tailor-made suit. On instinct, her senses lashed out and grabbed the woman, jerking her to attention and silencing her instantly. The woman's eyes went wide a heartbeat before she crumpled to the floor like a broken doll.

"Oh my god," her friend said with a gasp as she dropped to her knees and shook the woman who'd assaulted Jessie. "What did you do to her?"

"I didn't touch her," Jessie said. It was the truth. She hadn't touched the woman. Physically.

Before the woman could respond, Zack grabbed Jessie by the

hand and dragged her forward towards the courtroom. Anxiety poured off of him like a fog, making it difficult to breathe until she shook off his grip and fell into step behind him. He wanted to ask her what happened to the protester, but he didn't want to acknowledge that what she'd told him was true. To most people, shit like that just didn't exist.

Chapter 3

It took Zack ten days. Ten days, three hours, and five full re-charges on her MP3 player, but he did it. Jessie owed him big time. She was free. Mostly. She'd been released from prison and declared innocent, much to the outcry from the friends and family of the 'victims' in the community center. She gave about as many fucks when it came to their rage as they had given for hers. So, yes, she was free. But, she was still homeless and penniless in a small town full of people who wanted her dead.

"At least it'll be autumn soon," she said as Zack pulled into the parking lot of the cheap motel he'd been slumming in since he'd taken on her case.

"What's that?" he asked as he put the car in park and shut off the engine.

"It getting cooler out lessens the chance of dying from heat exposure," she said with a shrug as she climbed out of the car and shut the door. "Thanks for the ride."

"Where are you planning on going?" Zack asked her as she stuffed her hands in her jeans pockets and looked down at her boots. He'd brought the backpack filled with the few meager possessions she'd had left to the court house every day of the trial, just in case. But, the only things she'd opted to change into were her jeans and her trusty boots with 6" chunky heels.

"I don't know," she admitted. "With my prime suspects smoldering in Hell, I don't have any other leads on where Daniel is. But, I have to find him. Or, die trying."

"Are you sure he's your sister's son and not yours?" Zack asked her, making her cringe.

Her fraternal twin, Teresa, had told every lie she could to the people in town to preserve her reputation as being the put-upon saint with the damaged sister. When Teresa had gone and gotten knocked up at the age of 16, she'd even gone so far as to say Daniel was Jessie's bastard and she'd missed so much school because she'd had to take care of her during the pregnancy. Too bad Jessie was still a virgin and actually the caregiver in that equation.

After Daniel was born, Teresa made it a point of staying as social and active in her church groups as she had before she'd become a parent. That left Jessie to take care of the baby. Their mother wasn't much help. After their father had passed away, their mother had found her comfort in the bottom of a Johnny Walker bottle with a Prozac chaser.

Jessie had dropped out of school to care for them both as best she could. The benefit checks the Army sent every month had helped. It was rough, but Jessie had embraced the responsibility with open arms. Daniel had helped her find her center. But the brief happiness she'd found in the innocent acceptance of her nephew's love hadn't lasted.

"He's all I have," she said quietly, trying not to break down again. Zack had refilled her prescription on the way back from the courthouse and she'd dry swallowed her normal dose. But thinking about Daniel was still too painful. She couldn't shake the nagging feeling that there was something she was missing.

"And what are you going to do if you find him?" Zack asked as he came around to her side of the car and put his hand on her shoulder. It was kind of him not to point out that he'd been missing for almost a year. Or that the chances of finding him alive were next to nothing. Holding out the hope that she might find him healthy and in one piece was the only thing keeping her going. "High school drop outs don't exactly have bright futures in this world, especially with a kid to take care of."

"He's about to turn six soon," she said. "I can find something part time while he's at school to make ends meet."

"I think I have another option for you, if you're open to hearing it," he said, making her frown.

"What are you, some kind of angel of mercy?" she asked sarcastically. In her experience, nothing ever came for free. He'd flown in from Las Vegas and stayed with her throughout the trial for free. *And* he was thinking about her future? His kindness, though welcome, had to come with a hefty price. "Or are you going for sainthood?"

"Something like that," he smiled. "Come with me. I have someone I want you to meet."

Jessie sighed and made a sweeping gesture with her hand, silently telling him to lead the way and adjusting the canvas backpack on her shoulder. He smiled in triumph and led her up the rickety concrete steps that connected the ground level to the outside balcony of the second floor. He swiped the keycard through the reader, popping the lock on his door, and pushed it open with a grunt.

The room was something out of a 70's skin flick, complete with moldy shag carpeting and the signature scent of the dusty AC unit set into the wall under the window. She briefly had an image of him dropping trou and telling her to meet his dick, but movement in the corner of the room caught her attention. A man was standing next to the bed with a Bible in his hand, flipping the fragile parchment pages carelessly with a slight smirk hovering at the edge of his thin mouth.

Recognition flared as he lifted his dark brown eyes to the door and a charming smile broke out in earnest. Jessie knew him from somewhere, but the image was just an echo and blurred by stress. He tossed the bible on the bed and walked straight for her.

"Jessica Mead," the man said, crossing the room with the aid of an antique black cane topped with an ornate silver handle. "It's a pleasure to finally meet you in person."

"Jessie," Zack said as the man came closer, holding out his hand for her to take. "This is."

"Elijah Bernal," she finished without a pause as her thoughts clicked into place.

"Correct, my dear," Bernal said as they shook hands briefly. "But, please, call me Bernie. All of my friends do. Zadkiel, I knew our young friend here was powerful, but you never told me she was so stunning."

"Zack, please, Bernie," her attorney said with a note of slight irritation. "And, I didn't think that was important."

"The beauty of the world should be protected above all treasures," Bernal said in mock chastisement.

"Would you not help her if she were ugly?" Zack asked.

"Right here, folks," Jessie reminded them.

"Of course I would," Bernal said as if she hadn't spoken and then turned to her. "And, congratulations on your exoneration, my dear. You have your freedom and the world in front of you. And, if I understand correctly, you are in the unique position of having nothing to prevent you from moving forward with your new life."

"If that's how you want to put it," she said quietly.

"Have you thought about your future at all?" Bernal asked in a chipper tone as he turned away from her and sat at the small table against the wall, gesturing for her to take the seat across from him.

"A bit," she admitted darkly as she slid into the cracked Naugahyde chair and set her backpack against her leg. She kept her body turned slightly, prepared to make a break for it if she didn't like what the old man had to say. "Why?"

"Well, I wanted to talk to you about a possible course of action," he said with a knowing smile. His eyes seemed to analyze her position and he approved of what he saw.

"If it has anything to do with me getting naked for money in any way, shape, or form, I'm out of here," she said bluntly.

"Oh, no, my dear," Bernal said with a chuckle. "Quite the opposite, actually. You see, I am the head of a place called the Institute of Mercy."

"And, that's my exit cue," she said and got up from her chair without hesitation. "I've had enough religious nuts to last me ten lifetimes, so thanks, but no thanks."

"Not mercy," Zack said, moving to block her exit. Heat crept over her skin as she eyeballed the man who'd just saved her life. He may have been bigger than her, but she wasn't about to stay trapped in a crappy hotel room with a couple of Jesus Freaks. "M.E.R.C.E. The Institute of Modern Education and Research in Channeling Energy."

Jessie tilted her head back slightly, inhaling deeply as she drew in the feeling in the air, testing it for deception. Nada. She narrowed her gaze on Zack first, then turned to Bernal. "Do what now?"

"I've done my homework on you, my dear," Bernal said with a mischievous smile. "Constant reprimands in school for violence, though no one could prove that you were directly involved in any of the accidents. And all of the children who were directly involved were guilty of bullying, be it against you or not. A history of mental instability and a diagnosed schizophrenic. Yet, you seem to be the most well-adjusted, normal member of your living family. Especially when one takes into account the events that caused you to grow up so quickly."

"So?" she asked getting irritated. "All that tells me is that you managed to get your hands on my medical files, which is a felony, by the way, if you got them without consent."

"Bah," Bernal said with his ever present smile intact. "People like us tend to operate on a different level where the law is just a suggestion to keep our names out of the papers."

"People like who?" she asked as she adjusted her backpack on her shoulder and crossed her arms over her chest.

"Like you and I, my dear," he said in a tone that sounded like it should have been obvious. "Energy Mancers."

"It sounds like the only thing you and I have in common is that we're both crazy," she said. "You want to compare meds?"

"I'm being serious, my dear," Bernal said as his smile started to falter.

"So am I," she shot back. "Energy Mancers? Really? You sound like a nerd playing Dungeons and Dragons. Zack, thanks for the lifeline, I owe you big time for it, but even I can't handle this much crazy in one day."

"Jessie, please, just hear him out," Zack said as he continued to block her exit. "It's not as crazy as it seems."

"Bullshit," she said with a roll of her eyes.

"We can help you find your nephew," Bernal said. That got her to stop. With her heart in her throat, she turned around to face the man who'd regained his smirk. "If he's still alive."

"How?" she asked, hating that she was buying into the line, but too desperate to care. An image of Daniel's bright, unassuming smile and messy dark hair floated to the surface of her mind on a wave of intense loss. She'd sell her soul to get him back safe and sound.

"In a world where myth and magic are as real as you and I, anything is possible. All you have to do is take the leap of faith and trust me," he said gently. "At MERCE, there is an entire world of powers and abilities just waiting to be discovered. We teach people like you to harness the powers they were born with and use them to achieve their goals. We even teach mundane trades and skills that they can incorporate their abilities into, allowing them to live normal, well-paid lives with their families after graduation. Imagine having your nephew with you, full-time, with a guaranteed career and income to ensure his future as well as your own in whatever field you choose. All you have to do is agree."

"So, if I go with you, to this 'school,' and play along with the whole fantasy thing, you'll help me find Daniel," she said. It wasn't a question. She could give a shit less what education or job placement he offered. All she wanted was Daniel back.

"Of course," Bernal said, smiling wider.

"Where do I sign?"

Chapter 4

Jessie pulled her knees up to her chest and hooked her heels on the edge of her seat. She stared out the plane window at the mountains passing below and sighed. She was still fighting the internal war between her head and her heart. After she'd agreed to buy into Bernal's delusion, he'd slipped her a plane ticket out of Dallas to Denver and left. She'd changed her mind almost as soon as the door had closed behind him.

She'd run through the logistics in her mind until she'd given herself a splitting headache. It had taken hours, but Zack had listened quietly while she fought with herself out loud. If Daniel was still alive, every second she wasted with whatever cult bullshit Bernal was pedaling took her farther away from keeping him that way. There was no telling what kind of danger he could be in or what could happen to him if she left him there. On the other hand, if he really was lost to her, she'd spend the rest of her life chasing his ghost. She hated herself for it, but her instincts were telling her to go.

"I don't know what to do, Zack," she'd said as she flopped down on the end of the bed and buried her face in her hands.

"The only one who can make the choice for you is you, kid," he'd told her. "What was it your dad used to say?" he asked, but she knew he remembered. She said it all the time.

"Hope for the best but prepare for the worst," she'd said.

"So, look at it like this. Best case scenario, Daniel is alive and well, waiting patiently for you to come for him. You go to MERCE, learn to control what it is that you do and use it to find him. You get your family back and you can finally move on from this Hell."

"And, the worst case?"

"Worst case is he's already dead," he'd said bluntly, making them both wince. "But the people at the Institute can help you find his remains. You could finally put him to rest, and your pain along with him. Maybe then you'll be able to move on and do some good in the world in his honor."

"I can't just give up," she'd said quietly as guilt lanced her chest. Giving up was too selfish.

"You're not," he'd said as he put his arm over her shoulders in comfort. Paternal love and concern flowed through him so easily, it made her wonder if he had kids back home.

"But, what if he's here?" she'd asked again.

"If he was," Zack had said, making her look him in the eye, "you would have found him by now." When she sighed and shook her head, he dropped his arm and looked at the TV without really seeing it. "You remember when you were a kid and you used to play hide and seek with Teresa?" he'd asked.

She'd looked at him with her brows furrowed. She'd told her therapist the story, but she hadn't realized he'd read the file. "Yeah. She always accused me of cheating."

"Because you always found her," he'd said.

"Because the voices told me where to look," she'd said.

"Your instincts told you where to look," he'd corrected her. "You have a gift, kiddo. Your instincts are dead on. When you set your mind to something, and you listen to your gut, nothing can stop you."

"You sound like my dad," she'd told him.

"He sounds like a smart guy," he'd said with a slight smile. "And, I think he'd want you to go."

Jessie had cringed at the thought and fallen backwards on the squeaky mattress, staring at the ceiling and rubbing her knuckles against her sternum in an effort to keep her tears at bay. She'd never been comfortable with overt expressions of emotion and the idea of breaking down in front of her attorney helped her keep herself in check.

"Sleep on it," he'd said as he gathered his suit coat and bag from the other bed. "The room is paid to the end of the week, so you're welcome to stay."

He must really have been going for sainthood.

"Call me if you ever need help," he'd said as he pressed a wad of bills and a cell phone into her hands before he left. She'd nodded and locked the door behind him. After that, she'd spent the next three days and nights chewing on what he'd said and staring at the ticket Bernal had given her.

When the end of the week came, she'd grabbed her backpack and started hitchhiking to Dallas before the dawn had fully broken on the horizon. Zack was right. If she didn't do something, her psychosis and pain would consume her until there was nothing left. She'd never handled being idle for too long very well. And whether her nephew was alive or not, she was going to need help finding him.

"Miss?" a sweet voice asked, breaking her reverie. Jessie looked around in confusion as she realized the plane was empty.

"Sorry," she said quietly and scooted past the flight attendant with her backpack in her hand.

She kept her head down as she walked through the terminal. The paper Bernal had included with her ticket said to go to the north side of the building and await transport. She kept her head on a swivel as she moved. She wasn't sure how far the story of her trial had gone, but she really didn't want to chance it. The last thing she wanted to deal with was a lynch mob in the middle of the airport.

When she got to the baggage claim area, she had no idea where to go. The signs at either end proclaimed where cabs and rental cars were available, but there was nothing about public transportation to MERCE.

With a groan of frustration, she approached the service desk and found a young blond painting her nails and popping her gum.

"Can I help you?" she asked in a tone that had Jessie's fingers itching with the urge to reach out and touch someone. Hard.

"I'm trying to find the bus to MERCE," she said after taking a deep breath. "It's a school."

"You're joking, right?" the girl said with an exasperated expression.

"No," Jessie said shortly.

The girl rolled her eyes hard enough to make Jessie wonder if her retinal nerve was double jointed and turned to the computer. Her acrylic nails clacked away on the keys. "There's no bus to mercy today."

"When is the next one?" Jessie asked. Bernal hadn't included a ticket with the information he'd given her. If she'd missed the last one, she figured she could stay in a hotel for the night and leave the next day.

"There ain't no busses to mercy, lady," the poster-child for customer service said, chomping her gum in such a way that it popped and snapped as she gave Jessie a "fuck you" grin. "No place called mercy around here, either."

"Great," Jessie said with a sigh.

Don't give up, the reasonable voice whispered, making her twitch involuntarily. *Follow Bernal's instructions.*

Fuckthisbitchfuckthisbitchfuckthisbitch

"Shut up," she whispered.

"Excuse me?" the girl asked in a voice just shy of a shriek. "What the hell is your problem, lady?"

"Nothing," Jessie said and shook her head as she turned away from the counter.

"Yeah, that's right, walk away," the girl said in a haughty tone. "Freak."

"What did you say?" Jessie asked, turning back around with narrowed eyes.

"You heard me," the girl said in the same tone.

Jessie was tired, hungry, and pissed off at being lost with no other help than the voices in her head. This bitch was just the cherry on top of her shitty mood. Jessie calmly walked back to the counter and leaned on her arms to get in the girl's face. With a sadistic smile, she reached out and grabbed ahold of her mind, pressing an image of her reaching out and snatching her by the hair into the blonde's frontal lobe.

"You need to learn that there are some people in life you do not want to fuck with, Madame," she whispered as the blonde's brown eyes peeled wide. Without moving a muscle, she twisted the image and all of the physical sensations that went with it. The girl's greatest fear swam to the surface with her pain. She was afraid that her job would be the death of her. Knowing that, Jessie made her believe she was slamming her face repeatedly into the keyboard, breaking every bone in her face viciously. The girl croaked out loud while she screamed in her mind.

When the girl's brain believed that her teeth were embedded in the keyboard and her face was mush, Jessie let go of the image but not her mind.

The girl slumped in her chair as soon as she let go. She stared at Jessie like she was the devil incarnate. "Life is short, sweetheart," she whispered. "Your attitude will only serve to make it shorter." Jessie smiled as she passed out and hit the floor.

"Excuse me, miss?" she asked in an innocent voice as she leaned over the counter and pretended like she cared. When the girl didn't answer, Jessie went to the nearest person that looked like they worked there and pointed her out on the floor.

In the flurry of activity that followed, Jessie simply walked through the doors to the loading area and into the blinding sun. She raised her hand to shield her eyes and breathed in the fresh air. A part of her relaxed after the outburst, like a beast satiated by a full belly. It made it easier to think of what her next move should be.

"That was bloody brilliant," a female voice with a thick British accent said. She turned and saw a leggy young woman with smooth skin the color of dark chocolate smiling brightly at her. She was leaning against the wall beside the sliding doors twisting a thin purple braid around her finger.

"Huh?" Jessie asked, looking around her to see who the woman was speaking to. "Me?"

"No, the other Mancer behind you," the girl laughed. The duh was implied. "I've never seen someone actually manipulate another person's energy like that before. How did you do it?"

"How do you know I did anything?" she asked with a challenge in her voice. She'd never been praised for that kind of behavior before. Everyone who'd suspected her involvement usually called her the devil and feared her for it.

"Don't get touchy, love," the girl said. "Mancers can feel when others use their powers nearby. It's like a homing beacon or something. Cat's out of the bag, gorgeous."

"You're a Mancer," Jessie said. It wasn't a question.

"That I am," the girl said proudly.

Jessie tilted her head as she took her in fully. She was almost a head taller than Jessie, even with her heels on, and built like a supermodel; long legs, thin frame, nice tits. She was dressed comfortably enough in jeans, high-tops, and a tank top that read "Nerdy, Dirty, Inked, and Curvy," though the way she carried herself made it seem like her style was more high fashion Milan than comfy.

But, it was her eyes that held her. They were pale grey, standing out in startling contrast to her dark skin in a way that almost made Jessie squirm.

"I'm Chantel," the girl said, holding her hand out in greeting. "Chantel Wilson." Jessie shook her hand briefly, looking at her in question. "This is the part where you tell me your name."

"Jessie," she said as she absorbed as much as she could about the girl. "You're on your way to MERCE?"

"Are you a clairvoyant?" Chantel asked honestly.

"Not really," Jessie said with a raised eyebrow. "I was just hoping to catch a ride if you're headed that way. Bernal said to go to the north side of the building, but he didn't say what I was looking for."

"Who's Bernal?" she asked, her accent making it sound more 'Oo's Bernal.'

"Just the guy that recruited me," Jessie said. "Where are you from?"

"Bedford," she said with a smile. "England, love," she added when Jessie didn't react.

"I know where Bedford is. I was just curious," she said. "So are you going to MERCE or not?"

"I am," she smiled. "New student. Mum and Dad were oh-so-relieved when the guidance counselor of my last school approached them with the option. I'd already been through ten private schools already. Regular University wasn't really an option. So, it was either work or MERCE. I'd never been to the States before so," Chantel said as she turned away from where Jessie stood to retrieve her luggage.

"Wow," Jessie said with a laugh. Chantel was sporting a three piece set of Prada luggage with a matching trunk, making Jessie painfully aware of the humble wad of charity in her pocket. "You need help with that?"

"Oh, thanks, gorgeous," Chantel said with a wide sparkling smile. She handed Jessie a duffel bag and the handle of her rolling trunk. "I've been having any cute guy with a decent smile lug this shit around for me the whole way from London. It's nice to have help I don't have to flirt with. Not that it's much of a chore," she added with a wink.

"Where we headed?" Jessie asked as Chantel struck off in what felt like a random direction.

"My itinerary says the cars will pick us up on the other side of the building in ten minutes. I was just sitting on this side because there's more shade, but I'm glad I did. Otherwise I would have missed the show. You have got to teach me how to do that. Can you imagine? Anytime I run in to some catty little twat, I can just shut them down."

Chantel continued to ramble the entire time they waited on the north side of the building, but Jessie didn't mind. She liked her accent and it was nice to talk to someone who didn't give two shits about her abilities, let alone be put off by them.

"You want one?" Chantel asked as she pulled out a pack of cigarettes from her jeans pocket.

"Are you old enough to smoke?" Jessie asked honestly.

"I'm nineteen," Chantel said preening. "Are you?"

"I'm 22," she said as she took one. She hadn't had a cigarette since before the trial. Somehow it felt like she'd get in trouble if Zack caught her smoking. "Got a light?"

With a mischievous glint in her eye, Chantel pressed her finger to the end of her cigarette and started to puff. Jessie laughed and shook her head in amazement as the end started to glow under her touch. When she was satisfied that it was lit, she did the same to Jessie's.

"You know," Chantel said as she sized Jessie up visually. "If there's a decent mall near the campus we'll have to go shopping. You've got a nice set of curves on you and that baggy shirt and jeans combo does not do it justice. We need to put those assets of yours on display properly," she said motioning to her chest to make sure she understood she meant Jessie's double D's.

Jessie listened as Chantel proceeded to plan out their next three free weekends with an absent smile hovering at the corners of her lips. She'd never tried to make friends before. But, with Chantel it was easy. She just kind of talked like they had been friends their whole lives and including Jessie in her thoughts was the most natural thing in the world to do. It was. Nice.

When a Range Rover pulled up in front of the building a half an hour later, Chantel bounced and clapped rapidly. Jessie turned to the car to see a white circle cut into four equal parts painted on the front door. Each quarter of the circle brandished one of the four elements with the letters M.E.R.C.E. curving under the bottom of the circle.

"Ms. Mead? Ms. Wilson?" a light tenor voice asked through the open window. Jessie leaned over to see a man with an impressive amount of ink and metal in his face smiling back at her. When she nodded, his smile got wider. "Thank God, I've been driving around for the last twenty minutes looking for you. I was afraid I'd have to call Luke," he explained as he undid his seat belt and got out of the car. "Hop in and get comfy, we have about a six and a half hour drive ahead of us after we stop and get something to eat. I'll get your luggage."

As he came around with his grin still in place, Jessie nodded in appreciative admiration. He was wearing a black shirt over dark blue, designer jeans, complete with a chain hanging from his hip, and tan work boots. The tattoos on his face continued down his neck to his sculpted, sinewy arms. They swirled with the natural curves in designs that felt ceremonious and traditional until there was more ink than skin. Large, open hoops stretched his ear lobes wide enough for her see straight through. His entire bottom lip and left eyebrow was lined with steel rings. It was hard to tell beneath the ink and metal, but if she had to guess, she'd say he was in his early thirties.

As he stepped up to Jessie to take her backpack, she looked up and shook her head. "I've got mine. These are all hers," she said with a gesture to Chantel's Prada.

"Ok," he said with a shrug and took the handle of Chantel's truck from her and dragged it to the back of the car.

"Sorry, we're late by the way," he said as Jessie carried the other three bags to him. "My sister just flew in, too, and she decided to wander around the shops instead of meeting me by baggage claim like I told her to."

"No worries," Jessie said with a shrug.

"Shotgun," Chantel declared and happily hopped into the front seat. Jessie opened the door to the backseat and climbed in next to another girl with flaming red hair and a sour expression.

"Hi, I'm Jessie," she said holding out her hand. She normally wasn't a very open person, but hanging around Chantel made her wonder if she could ever be that friendly.

"Reba," the red-head said curtly without shaking her hand. "Theo," she said in a whiny voice. "What's taking so long? I'm hungry. Can we go now?"

"Just a minute," the tattooed man grunted as he wrestled Chantel's trunk into the back of the SUV. "Calm your shit." Jessie had to bite her lip to keep from snickering at his snap response and his martyred expression.

She leaned over the seat and grabbed the handle of the duffle bag preventing Chantel's trunk from sliding in and lifted it onto the black plastic footlocker closest to the seat. "Thanks, beautiful," he said with a smile as he was finally able to push the trunk into place and close the hatch.

Jessie fought the blush that threatened to spread across her cheeks at the compliment, even if he was just being friendly. She hadn't even realized she could blush. When Reba sighed in disgust, Jessie's little bubble burst, bringing her crashing back to reality.

"Mmm," Chantel said with a purr from over the shoulder of the front seat as he came around. "I would do dirty things with him," she said before he opened the door, making Jessie laugh in earnest.

"What's so funny?" Theo asked as he closed them all in together and fastened his seatbelt.

"Our new recruit wants to fuck you the first chance she gets," Reba said with a sarcastic smile to Theo's reflection as he looked at them in the rearview mirror.

Completely unabashed by Reba's comment, Chantel leaned on the center console with her chin in her palm and batted her eyelashes with a sly smile. Theo laughed at her expression and shook his head. Jessie smiled again as she watched a slight blush creep through the ink on his face and a pair of deep dimples pop in his cheeks.

As Theo started the engine and pulled away from the curb, Jessie laughed to herself internally. Reba was sitting slouched in her seat with her feet on the bench between them. She was brooding as she stared with open malice at Chantel. It was going to be an interesting ride.

J.P. Hart

Chapter 5

"MERCE has been my home for the past six years," Theo said as he handed a cup of coffee to Jessie over the back of the passenger seat. "Black with sugar."

"Thanks," she said as she popped the plastic lid on the cup and inhaled the smell of liquid life and higher brain function. They'd been driving for about three hours on the highway before the green and white siren called them to the next exit with the promise of caffeine. "Why so long?"

"After I graduated two years ago, Bernal kept me on as an instructor. With a face like this, I can't exactly work in corporate America," he said with his easy smile intact. "Double caramel Frappuccino, no whip," he announced as he passed Reba her drink and a straw. "It's alright, though. I love it there and I love teaching."

"What classes do you teach?" Chantel asked as he handed her another plain cup with tea tags dangling from under the lid. The question was innocent enough, but the marathon flirting she'd been throwing his way made Jessie wonder if she was mentally making a class schedule.

"He's a Master Terramancer," Reba replied.

"Was I asking you?" Chantel asked with her eyebrow raised in challenge.

"What's a Terramancer?" Jessie asked, stopping the snide

exchange before it could gain ground.

"A Terramancer specializes in Earth energy. We go on to be anything from construction workers, to herbal healers, to farmers. There's even a few of my students who are hoping to join the military after they finish at MERCE to be a part of emergency search and rescue teams. Imagine a person with the ability to move a rockslide to find the people trapped below."

"Sounds useful," Jessie admitted.

"Sounds heroic," Chantel added.

"What other kinds of classes are there?" Jessie asked. She hadn't really cared about the education MERCE offered. She'd only been focused on what they could offer her to help her find Daniel. But Theo seemed to genuinely enjoy educating people on what they did. "And how do you learn to be a Terramancer?"

Theo laughed as they pulled away from the parking lot and back onto the street. "You don't learn to *be* a Terramancer," Reba said to Jessie, giving her a look that made her feel like she was being called a moron. "You just *are* one."

"What my bratty little sister means to say," Theo said, looking up in the mirror and glaring at Reba, "is that a Mancer's specialization isn't something that can be taught. The soul determines the element, not the mind."

"Huh," Jessie said as she sipped her coffee and thought of the times her abilities had manifested. She tried to reconcile what she'd done in the past with the four elements, but couldn't figure out which one they would fit into.

"Which one does Bitch Magic fall under?" Chantel asked as she blatantly eyed Reba over the seat.

"I'm an Aeromancer," she said sticking out her tongue and sipping from her straw.

"That's surprising," Jessie said as she looked at Reba curiously. She would have thought Reba would be a Terramancer like her brother.

"Why?" Reba asked with a disgusted tone.

"Well, Theo said it was soul that decided what your specialization was," she pointed out.

"So?"

"I didn't think gingers had souls," Jessie said as honestly as she could pretend to be.

Theo snorted as he took a sip of his coffee at the red light, and Chantel outright laughed at Reba's enraged expression. Jessie simply smiled and looked out the window.

"That seals it," Chantel said between giggles. "You are officially my new best friend, Jessie."

After Chantel quieted down, Jessie turned back to Theo and continued to pepper him with questions about MERCE and the Mancers.

"The world wasn't created by some omnipotent parent figure in the sky," Theo said shortly after Reba put her headphones on with a complaint about newbies and their history-hard-ons, "it was created when the energy of the Primal Source came into contact with matter. The Primal Source isn't sentient. It doesn't have a worship-me complex. It's simply raw energy. No one knows where it came from or why it came into existence, but it did. The collision of it and the matter it came in contact with began everything. Life was simply a byproduct of the runoff energy that was left over, and that life evolved over millennia upon millennia until it gained its own self-awareness.

"With the birth of awareness also came the knowledge of life's ultimate fragility which bred emotions and the instinct to survive. That instinct drove progress and adaptation in such a way that the different species of creatures began to emerge."

"Fascinating," Chantel said, though her tone said she was anything but fascinated.

"I know, right?" Theo said, happily oblivious to Chantel's boredom. "But, we'll fast forward to about 65 million years ago. Those that were able to tap into the energy of the Primal Source began to realize that the energy that created them could also be used to gain power. Wars were breaking out between clans and species in a quest to harness the power of the Primal Source. Those who craved chaos and destruction became known as the Legions."

"As in the Legions of Hell?" Jessie asked in a deadpan tone. If he wasn't serious she would have laughed.

"Kinda," he said with a shrug. "Their image actually inspired the depictions of Hell we know today."

"Great," she said sarcastically. She was beginning to wonder who the real lunatic was between them.

"Thankfully, the worst of them were trapped in the Void between worlds when the Veil was created."

"The Veil?" she asked, not sure if she really wanted to know.

"Seeing the Legions' careless destruction of the balance of power, a benign race of beings came forward to call a halt to the wars. They came up with a plan to trap the Legions and separate the world into two parts, one for the energy users and one for the mundane. They spread out over the surface of the Earth and tapped into the energy of the Primal Source to create the Veil, but its creation was so disruptive it caused a mass extinction event that pretty much reset everything on this side and the other.

"The race panicked. They were safely cocooned in the energy of the Primal Source when the Veil was created leaving them as the only ones left who remembered what it was like when the two parts were one. In the aftermath, they saw the destruction they had brought on both sides and vowed to never again act on such a global scale. Instead, they dedicated themselves to the maintenance of the Veil they created and helping both sides recover."

"Ok, now that my brain has turned to mush," Jessie said, swirling the last cold remnants of her coffee in the bottom of her cup as she tried to absorb the information. "Where do the Mancers come in?"

"Well, that one's an easy one. The maintenance of the Veil started to become too much for the benign race to handle alone, but they couldn't afford to lose their numbers to childbirth and rearing, so the males began breeding with humans."

"So, Mancers are grunts that were created as some kind of genetic experiment with, what, elves?" she asked.

"Close," he shrugged. "Angels."

"You've got to be shitting me," Jessie said with a mirthless laugh. "Isn't that a bit cliché?"

"Not really," he said. "Not when you remember that the name angel was something we humans gave to their race. The religious ideals, and images that come along with it, were of our design. Angels aren't the lapdogs they are in the Bible. They're the gatekeepers between the worlds and their children were our protectors."

"So the whole god and the devil thing?" Jessie asked.

"A gross over exaggeration of a domestic dispute between one group of angels and another. I think one of them made a bet with another that their kids were better and they could prove it. Other angels joined in on the fun and boom, New Testament. Now, that's not saying there isn't darkness and light in the world, but good and evil is simply a matter of perspective."

Jessie frowned as she polished off the swill in the bottom of her cup and stared out at the failing sun. "What was the bet for?"

"Hmm?"

"The bet, between the angels that started the whole cluster-fuck for shits and giggles. What was the prize?"

"No clue," he admitted.

Jessie spent the rest of the trip deep in contemplation. She'd been told her whole life by the religious nuts in her hometown that she was the seed of evil, devil spawn. If what Theo was saying was true, then that technically made them right. It was not a comforting thought.

"Wake up, ladies," Theo said about an hour after they'd fallen silent. "We're home."

The Range Rover breached the ridge of a mountain crest, facing due west into the sunset. Jessie blinked rapidly as she looked through the windshield ahead of the car. It wasn't because of the light. It was because of what she saw cradled in the valley below.

Tendrils of crimson, pink, and orange reached out to gently illuminate a vast property of open land covered in lush green and wild forest. In the center was a red brick and iron structure that looked like a cross between a luxury hotel and a college campus. The main building was six stories tall in the center with circular two story buildings attached on either side. What looked like a small village dotted the area just behind the shorter building to the north, and a collection of plain beige square shops decorated the space behind the building to the south. From what she could see, there was at least an acre of open field behind the building, rolling lightly until the slope took a sharp incline just behind a thick line of evergreens at the foot of the mountains.

"You guys don't fuck around," Jessie said as she studied the layout of the grounds.

"How so?" Theo asked as Chantel stretched and yawned.

"Nestled in the middle of nowhere, in an area that makes it nearly impossible to sneak up on the property," she said with a raised eyebrow at his reflection in the rearview mirror. "What did you do, recreate a medieval fort? Are there trebuchets in the back?"

"No," Theo said with a laugh. "It used to be a ski resort, but we made some modifications to make it self-sustaining. I honestly don't think defensibility was on the brain at the time," he said with a shrug.

"Huh," she said and sat back in her seat, chewing on her lip.

Why did it seem like she was the only one who thought about threat assessment?

Shortly after Theo pulled the SUV over the ridge and onto the downward slope of the road, the bumps and jerks of the dirt road faded into the lullaby of cobblestones. Jessie forgot to keep her expression in check as she stared with open awe at the simple elegance that screamed class and sophistication. The tall clear glass windows in the front revealed dozens of people milling around inside.

The only piece of décor that seemed a bit out of place was the no nonsense lettering above the main archway declaring the building as the Institute of Modern Education and Research in Channeling Energy. Theo drove the car around the wide, circular driveway until they stopped under a covered arch in front of a pair of large wooden doors.

After he threw the car in park, Theo turned around to beam with pride at Jessie. "Welcome to MERCE."

Chapter 6

"I have never felt more like a tourist in my life," Jessie said as she stood by the tailgate of the Ranger Rover. As soon as the car had stopped, Jessie had hopped out to stretch her legs and look around. Chantel had opted to stay in her seat to fix her make-up after falling asleep in the car. Reba just refused to get up.

"It could be worse," Theo said as he pulled Chantel's luggage out of the back and set it on the cobblestone driveway. "We could be in some secret squirrel base in the middle of the desert."

"Secret squirrel?" Jessie asked with an eyebrow raised. "Seriously? You couldn't pick cloak and dagger or hush-hush. You had to go with the secret squirrel."

Theo chuckled as his torso disappeared back into the SUV and came back out with the matching bags. "What can I say? I'm old school."

"Or a dork," Jessie pointed out as she claimed the larger of the three duffle bags and slung it over her shoulder beside her backpack.

"You don't have to carry this stuff," Theo said, looking at her in question. "Help will be out in a minute."

Jessie sat the duffle bag back down on top of the trunk, but kept her backpack in place. Chantel may have been alright with having random people doing her heavy lifting, but Jessie felt more comfortable carrying her own shit. She turned as the double doors to the building opened to reveal three people striding purposefully towards them.

At the head of the group was a woman with closely cropped pink hair and naturally bronzed skin. Her hands were stuffed into the pockets of her torn jeans, but she smiled warmly at Jessie and Theo as she came closer. Following in her wake was a waifish woman with silver blond hair and stunning green eyes. She was wrapped in a thin, long dress the color of the Caribbean Sea and seemed to float more than walk.

Reba burst from the backseat like her ass was on fire when the third person stepped through the door. He was about the same lanky height and lean build as Theo but gave Jessie the impression of being almost twice his age. He was also from the more conservative end of the spectrum in straight-legged khakis and a buttoned white shirt. But, what caught her attention was the greying red hair he kept neatly trimmed close to his skull.

"Daddy!" Reba said with a squeal as she leapt on the man. He laughed out loud as he caught her midair and spun her around. The touching moment struck her hard and she had to look away. It reminded her of when her father would come home from one of his deployments and do the same to her.

"Welcome back, Princess," he smiled as he set her back on her feet near the back of the Ranger Rover. "How was your summer with Mom?"

Reba made a noise of disgust in the back of her throat and waved her hand carelessly. "Boring," Reba said. "All she did was work at the flower shop. She wouldn't even let me go hang gliding with Marcus."

"Neither would I," the man smiled, much to Reba's displeasure. "I don't like Marcus."

"And Mom doesn't like hang gliding, so I'm screwed either way," she said with a pouty expression.

"Not necessarily," he countered. "If there's time this weekend we'll go up together."

Reba smiled and clapped her hands rapidly before skipping towards the door, stopping to hug the women before disappearing inside. She didn't even pause as a fourth person, a giant of a man, hung back just inside the frame. It was like she didn't even see him. Or, she just didn't care.

Jessie watched him curiously as his eyes followed her. In the shade thrown by the overhang, it was difficult to make out his details past the short dark hair, but she could see his eyes burning straight through her skull.

She felt trapped by the shade of red smoldering in the shadow as he continued to stare at her without blinking. The color was so bright it almost seemed to glow, but Jessie wasn't intimidated by it. She was fascinated. Her instinct was to approach him. Test the waters like she would with an animal.

"Don't mind Lurker Luke," the woman with the pink hair said as she stepped in front of Jessie, breaking the mental game of chicken and forcing her to look away. "He's not very sociable."

"Like an angry bear isn't very friendly," the blonde woman added. "This is Ann. I'm Lena," she said with a smile and held out her hand.

"Aquamancer?" Jessie asked as she took the hand she was offered and was overwhelmed by the cool, crisp scent of fresh water. Lena beamed in response and nodded her head.

"You're clever," the pink haired woman smiled. "Can you guess me?"

Jessie leaned closer to the woman and inhaled, but all she got was fresh soap and deodorant. She started to frown and shake her head as the woman smirked and held out her hand. Jessie reached for what she was offered but hesitated at the heat pouring off of her skin.

"Pyromancer," Jessie said as she finally shook her hand.

"Nicely done, niñita," Ann said, genuinely impressed. "So, how did you guess?"

"She smells like a babbling brook and your skin is hot enough to fry an egg," Jessie said with a shrug. "It wasn't hard to figure out."

"Ann's right," Reba's father said as he came over to where they stood. "You are clever. Most people can't name a Mancer's specialization just by meeting them. Unless they're of the same troupe. I'm Jacob."

"Aeromancer," Jessie said as she nodded in greeting.

"I'm not close enough to smell, nor have we made physical contact," Jacob said as he looked at her curiously. "How'd you figure that out?"

"Process of elimination," Jessie said. "Earth, water, fire," she listed pointing to Theo, Lena, and Ann in turn. "That and you're Reba's father."

"We might have to keep her after graduation," Theo suggested to his father as he looked at her with pride. "Might come in handy to have another Tracker on staff."

"You lost me again," Jessie said with a frown.

"Any Mancer can feel their own kind, but a Tracker is someone who can feel and correctly identify the specializations of other Mancers, no matter what their specialization is," Theo explained.

"With proper training and guidance, a Tracker can also identify the different signatures in a Mancer's energy well enough to literally track them anywhere they go. It's rare to find someone who has a broad enough range to be able to track anyone," Jacob said. "Usually you have to hire someone in the same troupe as the person you're looking for."

"The only Tracker we have on staff right now is El Diablo over there," Ann said as she jerked her chin towards the giant.

Jessie thought briefly about what it would be like to live that way, hunting people down for a living. She could see the appeal if it could be applied to non-Mancers. It would definitely make finding Daniel easier. "I'll think about it."

"Think about what?" Chantel asked as she finally got out of the car and came around to where they were standing.

"They're trying to recruit me before I even graduate," Jessie said with a laugh.

"Why?" Chantel asked, but it didn't really seem like she wanted to know the answer.

Jessie shrugged and Chantel let it go, instead busying herself with making everyone's acquaintance. When the greetings were made and everyone knew each other's name, Jacob turned back to the doors and called out to the giant hovering in the shadows. "Luke, come down here and give us a hand, will you?"

The man seemed to hesitate when Jessie looked back at him, but he unfolded himself from the doorframe and came forward. He was bigger than she'd anticipated, at least a foot and half taller than her if not more, and built like a brick shit-house. Intricate, dark grey latticework tattoos wrapped around his forearms and disappeared under the short sleeves. He wore a black t-shirt bearing an American flag with a squid monster standing in front of it dressed in a suit. As he got closer, she could read the words "Cthulhu for President. Why choose the lesser evil?"

Jessie had to bite her lip to keep from laughing out loud when she read it, but she couldn't help the smile that teased the edges of her mouth. He paused just outside the group and stared at her. She felt her heartbeat pick up the pace under his gaze, but it wasn't the normal precursor to her defenses going up. Instead she felt a tug, like there was a string tied around her spine and he was pulling it through her chest. She flinched and looked away from him.

Evidently satisfied with creeping her out, Luke picked up Chantel's trunk with all of her luggage piled on top like it was filled with helium and walked back inside without a word.

"Can you guess his specialization?" Ann asked, leaning in to whisper her question as Theo and Jacob grabbed Reba's truck between them and led them towards the doors.

"Being a dick?" Jessie asked and Ann let out a sharp bark of laughter. She didn't say anything else about it as they made their way inside. She wondered if she wasn't too far from the mark.

The next hour went in a blur of beautiful architecture and paperwork. She and Chantel filled out form after form before being given key cards with their pictures on them and then a tour, led by Jacob. He showed them the south building first, making sure they knew where to find the infirmary, the gym, and the laundromat, as well as a small convenience store that carried basic school supplies. The building also had a library-bookstore combination, a coffee shop, and a huge rec room filled with plush couches and all manner of entertainment.

As they explored the second floor of the north building, Jacob pointed out a handful of rooms where some of the offered classes were held. It was easy for Jessie to pick up on which troupes used the rooms the most often, just by the equipment scattered around.

The scorch marks and heat resistant material on the walls of the room housing all manner of burnable paraphernalia identified the Pyromancers' workspace. The Aquamancers had a room filled with human sized tanks of clear, clean water and a large drain in the center of the floor. But the Aeromancers and the Terramancers didn't have a room at all.

"Small breaths of air, gentle enough to blow out a candle, are good for precision work and testing your focus," Jacob explained when she asked why. "But novice Aeromancers have been known to kick up tornadoes and hurricanes when under stress if they haven't had enough training. We do our specialization training outside like the Terramancers."

"What's that room?" Chantel asked, pointing to an open door leading into a space completely devoid of light.

Jessie breathed deeply as she moved behind Chantel towards the door. The scent coming from inside calmed her to her bones as she approached. She couldn't remember the first time she'd encountered it specifically, but it made her a little woozy with relief as the constant ticks and nagging voices seemed to dissolve into nothing.

"What's that smell?" Chantel asked, waving her hand under her nose and making delicate sneezing noises as she tried to clear it out of her sinuses.

"Incense?" Jessie suggested, getting closer to the door to breathe it in. As she approached, her skin began to tingle pleasurably and she shivered. Jacob stopped her as she reached the threshold of the room, closed the door, and looked at her in alarm. "What?"

"What specialization do you think you have?" he asked, making her frown.

"I don't know," she said. "Why?"

He didn't answer her. Instead he herded them away from the room and back the way they came towards the main lobby. Dread crept over her skin as she thought about the distress on his face.

"Should I already know what my troupe should be?" she whispered to Chantel.

"I do," she said, making Jessie feel worse. "I'm more than likely a Pyromancer," she said proudly. "Every time my powers have manifested I set something on fire, so," she shrugged.

"Mancers all have a certain level of control over all of the elements," Jacob said ahead of them. "Because everything is interconnected, a Mancer can use them all, but their specialization determines where they are the strongest."

"So, I may not be a Pyromancer?" Chantel asked, deflating.

"Maybe, maybe not. The fires may just be a result of your strong personality and you'll have a different specialization," he said with a shrug. "We'll find out during testing."

Jessie wanted to ask what element would give her the ability to get into other people's heads and manipulate them the way she could, but as they got farther away from the dark room the voice in her head kept her silent. It was afraid, whispering incessantly that she needed to stay calm and stay low. She'd have to wait for the testing to find out.

Jacob finished their tour with an entire wing of small rooms filled with desks and a single white board at the front.

"Our primary mission is to teach novice Mancers about their heritage and how to control their abilities, but we also offer classes similar to what you'd find at any college with the added bonus of job placement programs after graduation. Many of the curriculums are run through correspondence courses with Ivy League schools all over the world and the credits can be transferred post grad to any school you want to attend."

Jessie chuckled to herself at the thought of going to law school or medical school when she was done at MERCE.

"What's so funny?" Jacob asked. He didn't seem mad or upset by her humor, only curious.

"I didn't even finish high school," she told him, looking at her feet when she realized how bad that sounded.

"A lot of students here didn't at first," he told her. "You're what 18?"

"22," she corrected him, a slight challenge creeping into her voice. People always guessed her age younger than what she actually was. She knew it was because she looked young, but she couldn't help the feeling that they guessed low because they doubted her intelligence.

"You're still young, though," he said, shaking his head and putting his hand on her upper arm where it was exposed by her shirt. Paternal concern flowed through where his hand rested and her chest seized. "There are programs available to help you get your high school diploma before you start taking other classes. You're a sharp woman. You can do it."

Jessie stepped out from under Jacob's hand and looked away. Concern pinched his handsome face, but he let his hand fall. Tactfully, he decided not to press her on the issue as he led them around the circular hall and they came out in the lobby again. He filled the silence by telling them about the history of Mancers and the Veil, but Jessie tuned him out until they reached the bank of silver elevators nestled between two grand staircases twisting gracefully down from the fifth floor.

"This is where I leave you," he smiled. "Until you're placed with your troupes, you'll be in temporary housing with the other novices. The dorms are co-ed overall, but you two will be bunking together for the next three days since you arrived together. Temporary housing is smaller than the troupe housing, but it should still be enough room for you both. Feel free to relax there or explore the grounds. The only area off limits without an administrator is the basement."

"What's in the basement?" Chantel asked.

"Just the boilers and some administrative offices," he said a little too easily. "Nothing all that interesting."

Jessie didn't buy it, but the idea of exploring Club Bureaucrat was enough to lose Chantel. Jacob gave them each a map of the grounds and showed them where their room was before leaving them by the elevators.

"I can't wait to see our room," Chantel beamed as she hit the call button for the elevator.

"Anything will be better than the last place I was in," Jessie replied. "As long as the shower is private and the mattress is soft, I'll be fine."

"Bad flat-mate?" Chantel asked as the doors slid open and they stepped inside.

"Something like that," Jessie said evasively. She was beginning to like Chantel a lot, but she wasn't sure telling her she'd just gotten out of prison was something she could do just yet. "So, what do you want to do now?"

"First, I want to change clothes," Chantel said as she stretched her long arms over head and twisted her back to crack it. "Then, I was thinking we could go on a scavenger hunt for cute boys." She gave Jessie a sly smile as the doors opened again on the second floor and they stepped off the elevator.

"What happened to your crush on Theo?" Jessie asked as they turned to the left. A low din caught her attention and held it as they entered the temporary housing dorm. The hallway was packed with students. Some of them looked fresh from high school. Others looked old enough to be their parents.

"I never said I had a crush on him," Chantel smiled as a boy close to their age brushed past them, openly eyeing Chantel with a smile of appreciation. She smiled back and gave him a flirty wave. "I just said I'd do bad things with him," she finished once she was done checking out her newest piece of eye-candy. "Monogamy is a dirty word in my book."

"There's another dirty word for that," Jessie said as they came up to their room and swiped her key card through the reader.

"Meh," Chantel said with a shrug and followed her into the room, immediately flopping on the full size bed closest to the door and taking off her high-tops. "I don't really care what people think of me. I am perfect the way I am."

"I wish I had your confidence," Jessie admitted and claimed the other bed by dropping her backpack on it. Someone had placed Chantel's luggage neatly against the wall that separated the bathroom for the sleeping area. For just a second, she wondered if it had been Luke. It wasn't exactly comforting to think he'd been in her room.

"I call dibs on the bathroom first!" Chantel said, hopping up from the bed as fast as she had claimed it.

Jessie let out a small sigh, but smiled at Chantel's theatrics. She seemed so positive and energetic, it was hard to think of her ever being down. Maybe that was what Jessie needed, someone who could keep her positive. She pulled her boots off and dropped them next to the bed before laying back against the mountain of fluffy white pillows. After a minute, she threw her arm over her eyes. The sun had gone down by then, leaving the ghostly linens hanging over the window blissfully empty of light, but the lamp beside her hurt her eyes.

All she wanted to do was relax for a little while, but the voices in her head taunted and laughed at her, making her grind her teeth. Images of the blonde and the blood spraying from her mouth mingled with the carnage of the community center as the voices sang twisted nursery rhymes in the voices of children. And above it all, she heard Daniel's voice calling out for her.

Jessie growled to herself and sat up to grab her backpack. She practically tore the lid off of her Thorazine with shaking hands and dry swallowed her normal dose. She pulled out the MP3 player Zack had given her and shoved her earbuds in hard enough to hurt.

As she dropped her bag on the floor, she saw a small blue light blink inside. With a frown, she reached for it and found the cell phone she'd been given. She hadn't heard it ring.

She hit the button on the side to wake up the screen and saw a little orange circle with a three in it in the corner of the little envelope. Curious, she touched the screen over the icon and read the three texts from Zack.

"I called the motel to make sure you were ok and they said you left. Are you alright?" read the first one. Next was "Did you decide to go to MERCE?" three hours later. The last one was just after she'd arrived. "I'm glad you decided to go. They can help you with more than just finding Daniel. I know you're resourceful enough to make it on your own, but I don't want you to be distracted, so I worked it out with Bernal. Go see him tomorrow and he'll take care of you."

Part of her wanted to just send back a thank you and do what he said to do. But, she couldn't help the question nagging at the back of her mind, so she sent back, "Why are you being so nice to me?"

His reply was almost instantaneous. "We take care of our own." Then, "You're family." Followed by, "Get used to it."

Jessie sighed and shook her head before sending back one last message and putting the phone on the end table and laying back against the pillows again. "Thanks. For everything."

The phone blinked again and she read his reply with a slight smile. "Anytime, kiddo. Now get some rest."

She knew she would have to pay him back at some point. Nothing was ever free or without conditions in life. But, at that point, she didn't want to think about it. With the medication starting to work and the fog starting to roll in, Jessie closed her eyes and surrendered to the oblivion.

Chapter 7

Jessie leaned comfortably against the mangled torso that formed the arm of her throne as she casually stroked the midnight fur of the hellhound beside her. The stench of rotting corpses was like perfume in her sinuses as she inhaled. At her feet, a man knelt with his arms bound in chains of darkness. His labored breathing pleased her greatly. It wouldn't be long before he broke. And how she *craved* his subservience.

"My beautiful avenging angel," she said with a purr. "Won't you burn with me?"

"Never," he said in a growl and started to struggle against his chains again. "I die first."

"Mommy?" Daniel asked as he stepped past the man and looked at her. "Mommy the monsters are coming for me again."

"Shush, child," she said soothingly as she lifted him into her lap and dried his tears with a bloody rag printed with a frowning T-Rex. "I'll protect you."

"Mommy? Mommy, where are you?" he asked as his tears began to fall in earnest. "Mommy. I'm scared."

"I'm right here, sweetheart," she told him as her face twisted in panic. "Mommy's right here."

"He's dead, Jessica," the man on the floor said as he lifted his head and pegged her with his cold red eyes. "He's dead, damn it. You're comforting a corpse!"

Jessie bared her teeth at the man and hissed as the stone embedded in her chest began to pulse. She gripped Daniel close to her breast and smiled sadistically as the darkness burned the man until he bled and howled in pain. The hellhound beside her growled in appreciation as she kicked the man over on his side. His blood joined the rivers of countless other victims as he twitched.

Satisfied by his agony, she turned back to her son to find his rotting corpse in her arms.

Jessie startled herself into an upright position in bed and wiped the sweat from her brow. Nausea curled in her stomach as the image of Daniel rotting in her arms still echoed in her mind. She was shaking so hard her teeth rattled and her face was wet with tears. Kittie still thumped in her ears from her headphones and she wrenched them out by the cord.

The sun was shining through the thin curtains over the windows. She'd slept through the night. More exhausted then when she'd laid down, Jessie threw her still clothed legs over the side of the bed and stood. Chantel was missing from the bed she'd claimed and the sheets were still neatly tucked in. She must have been out all night.

Jessie was fine with that. It was probably better that her new friend not be around when she had one of her nightmares. She knew she talked in her sleep when the terror gripped her. Olga had asked her a few times if she'd been dreaming of her nephew when she'd been in prison. Apparently, she'd called out his name more than once.

She needed a shower, she decided. And coffee. She needed to move. Moving always made her feel better. She made a mental note to see if Chantel had a spare pair of sneakers to go running in and shuffled to the bathroom. When she got undressed, the sweat in the fibers of her clothes made it feel like she was shedding her skin and she cringed.

She'd hoped to be able to wear at least the jeans again. The only other clothes she had were a couple other t-shirts and her court clothes. She was going to need to buy more if she didn't want to do laundry every other day. She turned on the water and stepped under the scalding spray with a groan of pleasure. The shower in the motel room had run rusty and left a film on her skin worse than the prison showers had.

The endless clean, hot water at MERCE was heaven in liquid form. Chantel had left some kind of expensive body gel and a blue poof on the side of the tub, but Jessie reached for the gold bar of Dial instead. She took her time chasing the suds over her skin, going over every curve and crevasse until she was pink and wrinkled from the water.

When she was done scrubbing her hip-length hair with the off brand strawberry shampoo she'd gotten from a truck stop in Dallas, she shut off the water and shivered. The cold air that rushed into the bathroom and up her towel as she opened the bathroom door did almost as much as the shower towards helping her feel human. All she had to do was brush the fuzzy slippers off her teeth and she'd be good as new. She hoped.

She pulled on the grey slacks from her trial and the t-shirt that smelled the cleanest before setting out to find Bernal's office on the first floor. It hadn't been difficult, she'd asked the first familiar face she'd seen, Theo, and he'd shown her without asking why. On the promise of joining him for breakfast after, he'd waved goodbye and left her standing in front of what used to be the manager's office when the institute had been a resort.

"Suck it up, buttercup," she whispered to herself and straightened her spine before raising her hand.

"It's cruel," a deep voice roared inside, making her pause. "Dangling something like that in front of someone is wrong."

Jessie heard another voice mumble through the heavy wooden door, but she couldn't make out what was said.

"So, she'll leave. Good riddance! She doesn't need your bullshit promises and false hope," the deep voice answered in a lower tone than before, but she could read the rage and distress.

More with the mumbling. She leaned closer to the door to try and make out what they were saying.

"Spirare don't need anyone! We don't *need* anything from anyone! No, I will not calm down."

Mumble.

"Fuck you, Bernie. And fuck your bonding bullshit."

The door swung open, making her jump back in surprise. She was already on edge enough as it was. Seeing Luke filling the doorway, glaring down at her, made her want to climb the wall behind her to get away.

Her instincts flared and she swallowed her reaction to flee. "What's your problem?" she asked instead, matching his silent menace with her own aggression. "Did I interrupt something, or do you just have a door fetish?"

He stepped through the door and leaned down into her face.

"I'd watch the attitude if I were you," he said in a low rumble. His voice carried the strange lilt of an accent he'd long since buried and his tone reminded her of the thunder of a distant storm. "You don't want to see my bad side."

"Is there a difference?" she asked, rocking up on her toes until their noses were almost touching. "I'm not afraid of you," she lied.

"You should be," he replied and she knew he meant it.

"The bigger they are, the harder they fall," she said.

"I could crush you with my bare hands."

She wasn't sure why, but his rage amused her.

"How cute," she said and kissed the very tip of his nose. He jerked back slightly in response and frowned at her in surprise. "Try it and I'll make you wish you were dead before you do."

"Is that Ms. Mead I hear putting you in your place, Mr. Interitus?" Bernal called from the open office behind Luke.

Instead of answering, Luke straightened his stance and glared down at her one more time.

"Watch yourself, focul iadului," he said before turning in his heel and disappearing through the door at the end of the hall. She was pretty sure she'd just been insulted. As she shook her head and took a deep breath to calm her nerves, Jessie turned to the open door and went in. *That was fun*, the malignant voice cackled. *Let's do it again sometime.*

Bernal was sitting at a large oak desk, covered in file folders and loose papers. He paused with a pen just above one of the documents, but his eyes were on her over the lenses of his wireless reading glasses. He was smiling like he was sharing a private joke with himself that pleased him greatly.

"I thought that was your voice I heard," he said by way of greeting before signing the document on his desk and closing the folder. "I'm so glad you decided to take me up on my offer."

"I haven't decided if I'm going to stay or not," she lied. She didn't like the way he was looking at her. It was like she was a prize he'd won at a carnival.

"Of course, my dear," he said waving his hand as if it really didn't matter if she decided to leave or not. "It's your choice whether you stay or go. This isn't a prison."

"No shit," she said and raised her eyebrow at him. She wondered briefly if he'd realized what he said and who he said it to. Either way it was true.

"I didn't mean to offend, my dear," he said with an apologetic expression.

"Fair enough," she said. "Listen, I know this is going to sound bad, but Zack said I should see you. I don't know what he set up, but I wanted to ask if there were any part-time gigs available here that I could do to earn some cash."

"Of course there are, but not to you," he said, his smile returning at full blast.

"Why not?" she asked, slightly offended. "Is it because of my record?"

"No, no, dear," he said as he pushed himself away from the desk and palmed his cane, groaning slightly as he stood from his chair. "You are not a criminal. A person is only a criminal in the eyes of the law if they have been found or plead guilty of a crime. You were declared innocent, so you have nothing to worry about," he explained as he crossed the room to a file cabinet against the wall and put the file he'd been examining away, only to retrieve another.

"Then why can't I get hired?" she asked.

"Because, I won't let them hire you," he said. "Zack is a very dear friend of mine, a brother really. He and I made a deal. If you want money to spend on whatever it is that you want or need, you will use the expense account that's currently set up under your name," he told her with a note of finality.

"I don't need anyone's charity," she said as the discomfort she felt the night before returned.

"It's not charity, my dear. It's family," he said with a shrug. "Zack has been a part of this institution much longer than I have. In that time he has sponsored many students financially. He looks at them like they were his own children," he said with a chuckle she didn't understand. "Your case is just one of many."

"I'd rather earn it myself," she said. "Let someone else who actually needs it have it."

"There are no other students enrolled here that he's claimed, my dear," he said with a rueful shrug.

"Yeah, but," she began but he cut her off harshly.

"But, nothing," he said. "This is not a debate."

She wanted to argue, but she clenched her jaw shut.

"Now," he said after a pause. "The matter of your accounts. For now, your badge will serve as a temporary debit card of sorts. When you make a purchase at any of the shops on campus, just swipe it through the reader at the counter," he explained with his smile coming back full force. "I've already ordered a card for you to use off campus that should be here by the end of the week, but that should do for you to get some new clothes and whatever else you want in the meantime. The balance is only $50,000 so don't go too crazy."

Jessie nearly choked as she stared at him in disbelief. "This is a joint account right?" she asked. "Like, there are a hundred other people, so it's really only $500 for each of us."

"No," he said, shaking his head as he went back to the papers on his desk. "Just you."

Jessie felt dizzy.

"Very well," he said with a nod. "Here's a list of recommended supplies and your class roster," he said as he handed her a thin stack of papers stapled in the corner. She looked at him in confusion. "I took the liberty of scheduling your High School Equivalency exam for the week after the testing. As well as a few classes I think will fit well with your specialization."

"I don't even know what my specialization is," she said as she looked over the roster. Most of it was standard general education stuff, but some of it made her frown. "Basic Defense and Weaponry? Meditation and Healing? What the hell do you think I am? And what is L.I.?"

"Those are the instructor's initials, my dear," he said. "Lucifer Interitus." She stared at him. "I believe you've already met," he said with a wink. It clicked.

"His name is Lucifer," she said in a deadpan tone. When he nodded, she laughed.

"It's not uncommon for Spirare to take on the names of angels," he said and she quieted down. He wasn't amused. "If I'm not mistaken the angel Lucifer was quite moved by Luke's gesture."

"Oh, fuck me," she said with a groan.

"I appreciate the offer, my dear," he said with a smirk, "but I don't think I'd be able to keep up. Now, if you'll excuse me, I have some business to attend to and I want to finish this before I leave."

He didn't look back up after that and Jessie left in a daze. Half the classes Bernal had enrolled her in were taught by the red-eyed bastard. It was way too early in the morning for that shit. She needed caffeine.

"Where did you get that?" Chantel asked as she snatched the class roster and shopping list out of Jessie's hand as soon as she sat down beside her with her tray of breakfast. Theo gave her a smile of gratitude as she handed him a coffee, silently repaying him for spotting her on the trip in.

"Bernal gave it to me," she said. Part of her wanted to snatch it back, but she decided to let it go.

"So that's why you wanted to see him," Theo said with a nod. "I'm glad he's looking out for you."

"Who is this guy," Chantel asked, "and why is he so important?"

"Bernal is the Head Mancer," a thin brunette sharing their small table said as she looked at Jessie with a strange mixture of awe and confusion. "He's a bit of a recluse when it comes to the students. I've been coming here for the last two years and I've only ever seen him at the major events."

"Then, who do you normally see when you need something?" Jessie asked. He didn't seem like the type to lock himself in his office and ignore the world.

"Dr. Jones," the brunette said. "He's Bernal's assistant, but he's the only one I've seen personally."

"All of these are university level courses," Chantel said. "You said you hadn't finish High School, so he must have you mistaken for someone else."

"Nope," Jessie said with a sigh. "He scheduled my High School Equivalency exam for after next week."

"Why the hell is the Head Mancer doing this personally?" Chantel asked, surprising Jessie with the jealousy in her voice.

Jessie glanced at Theo who subtly shook his head. All Jessie could do was shrug. Her instincts told her to keep her yap shut about Bernal's strange interest in her future. It would mean explaining how they met. Which would mean she'd have to explain Zack, too. And coming clean about her past. "I need to go to the student shops later," she said instead. "You want to come with me?"

"Shopping trip?" she asked, completely forgetting the jealousy that had speared her voice only moments before. "Hell yeah! Can Alexis come?" she asked, indicating the brunette.

"Sure," she said and the girl smiled brightly.

"I told you she was awesome," Chantel said, making Jessie smile. Jessie listened quietly to Chantel and Alexis chatting boisterously for a while, until Theo motioned with his eyes for her to follow him when he got up.

"How are you?" he asked once they were out of earshot.

"I'm fine," she said. "Why?"

"You looked like refried dog shit when I saw you this morning and I just wanted to make sure," he said. "I really hope you can be happy here."

"How much do you know about me?" she asked. The look in his eyes told her he knew more than he let on.

"Not much," he said. "But, I know you jump when anyone tries to touch you without permission. You stand like you're always on alert for an attack. You're willing to let other people steamroll right over you without a second thought and get nervous when someone is genuinely being nice."

"So?" she asked as she crossed her arms over her chest and hugged herself tightly.

"So," he said as he leaned down to get her line of sight back, "I know hard wired self-defense mechanisms when I see them. Look at me," he said gesturing to his face. "I got most of this before I came here. It was my way of keeping the world at a safe distance."

"What's wrong with trying to protect other people?" she asked, thinking about the people she'd hurt.

"I wasn't protecting them, Jessie. I was protecting myself," he exhaled sadly. "Look, the Terramancers are on the third floor. If you ever need someone to just talk to, let me know. We can just sit and I'll listen."

"Thanks," she said and nodded when he looked at her.

"Good. Now, go have fun with your friends," he said. He started to move like he was going to hug her, but then he thought better of it and just squeezed her shoulder instead. She patted his fingers and pushed a hint of reassurance through the contact out of habit. She'd done the same thing to Daniel when he'd hug her and tell her he was worried about her. He jerked slightly in surprise but said nothing as he walked away.

Chapter 8

That evening, after Chantel and Alexis finished dragging Jessie reluctantly through the shops insisting she buy everything they thought looked "cute" on her, Jessie sat on the edge of her bed and laced up her new tennis shoes. The yoga pants she'd bought were a bit long, but she'd forgotten to get sewing stuff to hem them. She'd been too busy putting back the armfuls of stuff Chantel kept piling on her, insisting she could never have enough clothes.

Everything she bought could fit in her backpack snugly. If she had to make a quick exit, she could.

She tucked the extra fabric of her pants into her shoes and pulled on a sports bra. She clipped her MP3 player to the inside of her bra between her breasts and slipped her keycard under the band. She'd been eyeing the open terrain of the sprawling back lawn of the property all day. Since Chantel had gone out in search of entertainment, she finally had a chance to run.

She hit the play button on the player and jogged down the steps to start her warm up. One of the purchases she'd made was a simple laptop with built in Wi-Fi and an iTunes gift card at the bookstore. The laptop was a requirement. The gift card was her only splurge. Before she'd gotten dressed, she'd spent about an hour finding new music to load on the little player Zack had given her.

"Resistance" by Muse drummed through her as she jogged through the halls to the main dining room and out across the communal seating area outside. Her braid swung freely behind her as she moved, bouncing off her sides. Once she passed the line of the village of shops and extra housing, she took off at a dead sprint. She felt free.

She'd always been fast as a kid, and keeping up with Daniel had kept her in shape. Damn that boy could run. She'd chase him through the park and around the acre property where her family's trailer sat until both of them were purple and puffing. She got lost in the memory of him as she bounded through the trees of the forest-line about a mile from the back of the school. The terrain was rockier than it was in Texas and the incline was making her lungs burn, but she loved it.

Her heart was racing and the cool August air made her feel alive. She ran until she felt like she would collapse and then she started to taper off. When she'd slowed her pace enough to stop without seizing, she leaned against a tree and breathed. "Never Let You Down" by Woodkid was thumping through her earbuds by then. It was about an hour down the line of her playlist if she remembered correctly. She needed to head back soon, but she wasn't ready yet.

She rolled her head back on her shoulders and looked up at the sky. It was so clear out there. The brilliant blue of the day was giving way to the night, leaving the velvet blanket of stars a vibrant shade dark sapphire. Looking up at the heavens, her heart let out a gentle sigh of longing. She felt like a piece of her was missing. She always had. Daniel had helped fill the emptiness, but his absence had only made it raw.

"You would have loved it out here," she said to the Daniel in her memory.

"Who are you talking to?" a deep voice asked, breaking through the music in her ear. With a start, Jessie turned and saw Luke approaching her warily.

"No one," she said as she took her headphones out and stuffed them in her cleavage.

"You shouldn't be out here alone," he said. She looked at his gym shorts and sweat covered shirt and raised an eyebrow.

"Were you following me?" she asked.

"No," he said, but he looked away. He was lying. "I was out for a run and I heard movement so I came to check it out."

"Uh huh," she said. "Look, don't worry about me. I can take care of myself."

"I know," he said more to himself than to her. "Just don't come out here alone. There're wild animals out here."

"I'm looking at a grizzly right now," she said with a smirk. She couldn't help the chuckle as he looked over his shoulder and then back at her with an eyebrow raised.

"Smartass," he said. In the moonlight she could see a smile teasing the corners of his cruel mouth.

"Takes one to know one," she said back with a shrug. He laughed. It was short and a little dry, but it lit up his face in a way that made her smile.

"So are you going to head back?" he asked as he took a step closer. "If you are, I'll go with you."

"And let people see us together?" she asked. His smile evaporated and she quickly added, "I wouldn't want to tarnish your reputation of being an unapproachable bastard."

"Forget it," he said and turned away to jog back.

She could kick herself. He was just trying to be nice. Shaking her head, she ran after him. He was already a good clip away when her pants leg caught on a branch and she went flying into the underbrush.

"Shit," she said with a groan as she clutched her ankle. It was already starting to swell. "Fucking god damn. Mother fucking Christ."

"You swear worse than I do," Luke said as he jogged up to her. "Thought a sailor had gotten lost out here."

"Ow," she said and pointed at her ankle.

With a hard exhale, he pulled a military pocket knife out of his sock and knelt down beside her as he flicked it open. She jerked back and pushed herself away on her hands as he reached for her.

"I'm not going to hurt you," he said gruffly, but she saw the injured expression flicker in his eyes before he turned away. She held still as he gently lifted her uninjured ankle onto his knees and cut the excess fabric from the cuff before doing the same to the other.

When he was finished, he carefully removed her shoe and used the stretchy fabric to wrap her ankle tightly. Satisfied with his field dressing he handed her the shoe and then lifted her from the ground without a hint of straining. She'd never felt tinier. His face was like stone as he carried her out of the woods and a myriad of emotions poured through her from where his calloused hand rested on her back.

She felt the hatred and aggression he showed the world, and the cold calculation of a hard life. All of it echoed her own. Including his loss and yearning for people he could trust.

"Luke?" she asked as they came to the edge of the trees.

"What?" he asked, looking straight ahead.

"I'm sorry for my comment back there," she said and pushed her honesty and remorse back through the connection. His step faltered slightly and he stopped just inside the tree line, staring at her in open surprise.

"How did you do that?" he asked.

"What?"

"Make me feel that," he answered. She bit her lip and clammed up. "Please," he whispered, but his mouth didn't move. Hope flickered dimly in him as he stared at her.

"I don't know," she said quietly. "I've just always been able to, as long as there's some physical connection. I get echoes, too," she continued as his hope grew. "If the emotions are strong enough I can feel memories."

"Do you know what troupe you belong to?" he asked, almost if he was too afraid to ask.

"No clue," she admitted. "I didn't even know what a Mancer was until a week ago."

"If I ask you to try something, would you let me?" he asked. She wasn't sure why, but her instincts told her to trust him. When she nodded, he set her down on the ground again and lifted her ankle in his hands. "I'm going to try and heal the sprain."

"How?" she wasn't afraid. She was just curious.

"Spirare have a specialization in Spirit. We're rare, exceedingly so, but I learned a long time ago that if the Spirare are near enough to one another, they can draw strength from each other to heal. They've even brought each other back from the dead if their bond is strong enough."

Before she could press him for more information, he cupped his hands around her ankle and squeezed. It hurt like a son of bitch at first, but as he closed his eyes and breathed, warmth flowed through his hands soothing her injury. It only took a minute or two, but when he was done, he unwrapped her ankle and smiled. It was healed.

"I'm a Spirare?" she asked as she looked at the unmarred skin in his hands.

"I think so," he said. "But, you'll have to pass the test to be sure." His hope bloomed to full light as he looked at her with a crooked smile and she couldn't help but smile back.

"I might actually have to stick around, then," she said to herself, but his smile faded and he let her go. He helped her to her feet and let her lean on him to replace her shoe, but he didn't touch her again. "What were you arguing with Bernal about this morning?" she asked as they walked back at a leisurely pace. His voice was echoing in his own head before he'd broken their contact.

"Nothing," he lied.

"Wow," she said, feeling like she'd been slapped. "Ok."

"What?" he asked as concern colored his features.

"Nothing," she lied, but couldn't bite her tongue. "I just thought I might have actually found someone who wouldn't lie to me," she said with a careless shrug as she replaced her headphones and blocked him out. "I guess you're just like everyone else, huh?"

She didn't wait for him to respond. She just took off at a dead sprint as fast as her feet would take her.

Chapter 9

Three days later, Jessie sat in the grass behind the institute and ran her fingers through the blades mindlessly with the sun still rising behind her. The other novices were chatting amongst themselves, speculating on what the tests would be. But, Jessie just enjoyed the fresh breeze and the sun's warmth. She closed her eyes, tipped her head back, and breathed in the fresh mountain air.

The days before the infamous tests began had been the most fun she'd had in a long time. The day after her run, Chantel had insisted they check out the spa. Twenty minutes of convincing later Jessie had gotten her first ever manicure and pedicure followed by a heated massage courtesy of a Pyromancer with very talented hands.

She'd been so relaxed, she'd even let Chantel convince her to get her first professional hair cut in years. Paying for someone to do something she could do herself seemed needless, but the temptation of being able to cut the number of hair ties she needed to bind her braid down from six to four was too tempting to ignore. She felt amazing afterwards and Chantel had insisted they keep it going as long as they could.

The morning of the testing, however, a predawn wakeup call had broken their streak of sleeping late and goofing off all day. The voice on the phone had been nothing more than a gruff instruction to dress for being outside and gather on the back lawn, but Jessie knew who it was. She hadn't seen Luke since their run in the woods, but she couldn't shake the feeling that he was watching her.

"You're not on a spa day anymore," he said darkly from only a few inches away from her ear, making her jump and open her eyes. The bastard was crouched next to where she sat. A smug smirk hovered at the corners of his cruel lips making a muscle in his chiseled jaw jump. She hadn't heard him get that close and the thought that he could sneak up on her like that was not comforting. "Get up and get in line."

"Hey, Neanderthal," Chantel snapped as she came up to where Jessie was standing up and brushing the grass off her pants. "Leave her alone."

When Jessie had gotten back from her run, she'd been so pissed off she'd wanted to hit something. Fortunately, Chantel had come back to their room with a bottle of Jack Daniels and a case of coke before she'd gotten the chance. Three More-Jack-Than-Cokes later, Jessie had told her why she was mad. Chantel, like a good friend, had declared Luke a scumbag and spent the rest of the night filling Jessie's head with all the different types of petty revenge they could exact together.

Irritation built in the twitch of his muscles as he stared at Chantel and, for an instant, she was afraid he'd hurt her. Jessie did something she never thought she'd do. She reached out and rested her fingertips on his bicep, bracing herself for the onslaught of rage she knew had to building below the surface of his skin. Electricity crackled up her arm and into her chest at the touch, and his aggression bloomed brightly in her mind before ebbing just as quickly.

Luke jerked and stared at her in disbelief for a heartbeat before he turned on his heel and left her standing there in shock. She'd only meant to break his attention long enough to diffuse the argument before it started. She definitely hadn't expected anything like whatever that was.

"What the fuck was his problem?" Chantel asked in a huff.

Jessie continued to stare after him as he found a place not far away from the Masters. "Let's just join the others," she said and steered Chantel over towards the other novices waiting anxiously for the testing to begin. There were at least a hundred people there, but she recognized them all from the second floor rooms near hers.

The Masters spread the novices out in a semicircle around them with their backs to the institute and faced them with clipboards in their hands. Luke stood apart from them, but faced the novices as well. Jessie cocked her head in confusion as she looked at him, but no one offered any hint as to why.

"For those of you who haven't met us before," Jacob said from the opposite end of the line loud enough for everyone to hear, "we are your troupe Masters. I am Jacob Lancaster, head of the Aeromancers."

"I am Annabeth Esposito, head of the Pyromancers," Ann said at the same volume.

"I am Theodor Lancaster, head of the Terramancers," Theo said next.

"I am Lena Harris, head of the Aquamancers," Lena said with a bright smile.

There was a pause for a few moments until Jacob looked over at Luke. He shook his head and Jacob stepped out of line to address the assembly.

"Today we begin the process of placing you with your troupes based on your specializations," he said. "Now, some of you have come to us from Mancer or Mancer-friendly families and already know what your specialization is. For you, this will simply be a chance to test your skills with the other elements in case you want to branch out later and flex those muscles. For the rest of you, this will be the first time you will have a chance to explore your abilities in a teaching environment."

"The five tests are pretty basic as far as skill is concerned," Theo said without a pause as his father relinquished the floor. "But they are highly specific to the elements they test for, so don't be afraid if you fail a few."

"What happens if we fail all of them?" Jessie asked and then bit her lip as Luke focused on her again.

"Then you're not a Mancer," he said making her heart sink.

"What Luke means to say," Theo said quickly as other novices seemed to have the same reaction, "is that not everyone who shows signs of being a Mancer is one, but that doesn't mean you don't have a useful skill set. Some Mundanes are just sensitive to the energies, but they don't have the strength to use it themselves outside of a few isolated incidents when the energy of the Primal Source is present in heavy concentration."

"Many of these people go on to fill positions within the organization and the community that play a vital role in our day to day lives," Lena said.

"Translation: burger flippers and janitors," one of the novices spoke up. A few people laughed, feeling the confidence of knowing they belonged at MERCE. Jessie, however, had to grit her teeth together and breathe. If it was for Daniel, she would slog through shit for a living. Without him to provide for, she'd rather shoot herself in the head than wait on some entitled asshole for the rest of her life.

"How long would we be allowed to stay after washing out?" she asked as seriously and strongly as she could. She would not break down in front of anyone, let alone the handfuls of people giggling like over privileged children at the poorer class.

"I doubt this is really going to be an issue at all," Jacob said, holding up his hands in a placating gesture.

"How long?" she asked again, turning her head to look at Ann. The Master Pyromancer struck her as a survivor, so she hoped she'd get a straight answer.

"I'm sure arrangements could be made under special circumstances," she started to say, but Jessie cut her off.

"How. Long," she said through gritted teeth as she locked eyes with Luke, neither of them flinching.

"You don't," he said bluntly and she exhaled. The morale of the assembly seemed to plummet at his words, but Jessie was actually relieved. Knowing that, her brain started churning over the possible scenarios and what she'd do if they happened.

"Thank you," she said and he nodded slightly.

"Let's begin," Luke snapped and all of the Masters visibly shook themselves out of the somber train of thought.

"First up is the Terramancer test," Theo said and then turned on his heel and sprinted away.

"What is he doing?" Chantel asked just as the ground began to shake beneath their feet.

About fifty yards away, the ground below Theo exploded upwards and curved like a thirty foot wave around him. He rode the rolling earth forwards, moving his hands gracefully as he called to more ground to keep him steady as he surfed forwards at a steady clip.

When he almost too far away to see clearly, Theo twisted hips and threw the wave of dirt to the side to bring him to a stop. He only paused for a second before riding his wave back to the group.

"When properly trained," Theo said loudly as he approached, "a Terramancer can bend the Earth to his will in ways most people could never imagine."

"So you want us to do that?" Chantel scoffed.

"Not exactly," Jacob said with a small laugh. "That was just Theo showing off. In this test, you will simply be attempting to manipulate the ground, even something as simple as lifting it a few inches."

"We'll be breaking off into groups of twenty, each of the groups for one of us," Theo said using his thumb to indicate the Masters and Luke. "We'll observe and note the results."

"Now remember," Lena said, "this is not a competition. This is just an evaluation of your skill levels and where your specialization is. We'll post your scores before breakfast each morning starting tomorrow."

"May the best Mancer win," Ann said loudly, making Lena glare at her. Ann laughed at her expression and then held up her clipboard. "Alright, novices, when I call your name, line up in front."

Ann listed off twenty names and then paired them with one of the Masters. When the first group headed off with Theo, she repeated the process for Lena, followed by Jacob and her.

Chantel had been called to Ann's group, and she waved happily as she walked to join them. Jessie couldn't help the pang of disappointment in being separated. She could have used the moral support of a friend. But, she couldn't begrudge Chantel's excitement. She didn't have as much to lose.

She looked around at the remaining novices who all seemed confused. Each one looked like they were the butt of a joke they didn't understand, and the longer they just looked around, the more irritated they got.

"What the fuck, man?" one novice swore before sitting down hard on the ground. "It's like getting picked last for dodgeball and then getting left in the parking lot."

Jessie rolled her eyes and marched up to Luke, who was standing just a few feet from the group.

He crossed his arms as she approached and followed her with his eyes until she stopped in front of him.

"Who do you want to go first?" she asked and the corner of his mouth twitched.

"How about you, focul iadului," he said with a smirk.

"What did you call me?" she asked, not sure if she should be insulted or not.

"Hellfire," he said and shook his head as he approached the rest of the remaining group. "Listen up," he said in a thunderous voice, "as far as I'm concerned, you all are a waste of my time. The only one among you that could actually be smart enough to learn anything is this one here." He jerked his chin at Jessie, making everyone else stare at her. She flinched away from the attention and moved towards the back of the group.

"What makes her so special?" a tall, slim brunette asked in a disgusted tone before turning back to Luke and batting her eyelashes.

"Because in the ten minutes I have been standing there watching you all," he answered with a surprising amount of venom in his voice, "she was the only one that figured out that I am the one administering your test today."

"But, you're not a Master," someone else pointed out.

"Are you sure about that?" he asked, moving through the loose bunch of novices.

"There are only four elements," the brunette said but she looked like she wished she could take it back.

"There are five," Jessie said as the pieces clicked together. He said Spirare specialize in Spirit. Spirit was an element, too. It just wasn't tangible.

"Exactly," he said as he continued to weave through the group. The novices all shifted uncomfortably under his intense gaze. "Now, in case you haven't already figured it out," he said in a tone that made it clear he knew no one had, "the testing groups were drafted based on the specializations that have already been observed. You all have none, which is why you are with me."

"So, you're not a Mancer?" the brunette asked.

"He is," Jessie said quietly, she could feel the power rolling off of him like a physical caress. She'd thought she'd only breathed her response, but Luke's attention snapped to her anyway. His eyes narrowed briefly before he made his way out of the group again.

"Line up," he snapped. When everyone was done scrambling to

comply with Jessie going last so she could watch those ahead of her, he brought everyone forward one at a time. And, one at a time, every one of them failed to move even a pebble. Jessie watched in the distance as Theo's group manipulated the dirt into statues of varying complexity, while the other group occasionally managed small hills here and there.

When her abilities had manifested, it had always been a reactive response. And, she'd never moved earth before.

"Jessica," Luke said briskly, bringing her attention back to him. "You're up."

She took a deep breath and stepped up to the area in front of him. She closed her eyes thinking about the ground shifting beneath her feet, praying that she would succeed. She concentrated on an image of Theo surfing his wave in her mind with her heart hammering in her chest.

Nothing happen.

"I don't know how to do this," she admitted, looking up at him with a pleading expression.

"Learn," he said and clamped his jaw shut tight enough to make the muscle in his jaw twitch.

You can do this, the reasonable voice whispered. *Just focus.*

"It'd be easier if you wouldn't distract me," she whispered.

"What?" he asked in a harsh tone.

"Not you," she said shaking her head. "Nevermind."

She closed her eyes and tried again, willing the dirt to move, even just a ripple. She stood there, feeling Luke's growing impatience, fighting with herself to figure it out.

Again, nothing.

"Enough," Luke said and Jessie's heart fell.

"No," she said and grit her teeth. "Just let me try."

"I said enough," he said and came towards her, coiled in anger and frustration. For a split second, he looked like he was going to strike her, but a split second was all it took. Triggered by the threat he posed, her survival instincts kicked in, still focus on moving the ground.

A solid wall shot up between them in the blink of an eye, curling protectively over her as she crouched down and covered her head. She wasn't sure how, but she did it.

She lifted her head to see Luke calmly stepping around her shield, eying it carefully. Slowly, she got to her feet and looked at her handiwork.

"Does this mean I'm a Terramancer?" she asked quietly.

"No," he said, pegging her with a hard stare. "It doesn't mean anything."

Chapter 10

By the time the fifth day rolled around, Jessie was making a mental check list of all the things she needed to pack. The rest of the tests had gone much the same way the first one had. Luke loomed while she failed to summon enough wind to hover a few inches off the ground. Or redirect a stream of water as it was poured out of glass pitcher. Or light a fire in a bowl without matches.

When the first result posting went up, Jacob had explained how they were determined and what they meant. It was a simple point system; 2 points for a successful manipulation, 1 to 10 points for speed in success, and another 1 to 10 points for control. A novice that scored 10 or more points in one specialization would go on to be placed in that troupe. Easy enough for those that actually had a clue.

Sure, she'd successfully manipulated earth, but she needed at least 10 points in at least one group to be considered a Mancer and be able to stay. Theo had shaken his head sadly when she asked if she'd be with his troupe before she saw her name on the lists.

"Because it was reactive," he'd said, "and not your conscious choice, all it showed was that the potential is there, not a specialization. You only got the two points for the success, but we couldn't measure for speed or control. I'm sorry, Jessie."

She'd tried not to react, but her face had fallen an instant before she could turn away. Theo had been kind, trying to comfort her by reminding her that the potential was there, she just had to find her niche. But, it hadn't helped much. She was flying blind and she hated that feeling.

The stress of wondering what the future would hold made it impossible to sleep without her Thorazine, but she was too afraid to take it except for before the tests. If she washed out, she'd loose her access to the on-site counselor that she'd met after her spa day with Chantel, Dr. Jones.

He was primarily Bernal's assistant, taking care of the day-to-day face time with the students and staff, but he'd met with her to discuss her mental health. Apparently, in the mundane world, he'd been a trained psychologist, but he'd given up his practice and come to MERCE as a favor to Bernal.

The one time they'd spoken face to face, it was like talking to a meat puppet. He'd shown no expression or even seemed to have an original thought during their discussion. He hadn't asked about what landed her in prison or even Daniel, though she'd mentioned him at least once. He just sat and stared at her, barely blinking as she talked. It creeped her the hell out.

But, in the end, he'd agreed to keep seeing her and promised to make sure she got her prescriptions when needed.

If she had to leave the institute, that promise would be null and she knew she'd eventually run out. The idea of going back to the incessant noise in her head made her nauseous. Even if she managed to find Daniel, without help she wouldn't be in any kind of condition to take care of him properly. That was the danger of getting care just long enough to get used to it.

With a heavy sigh, Jessie stuffed the last of her clothes into her backpack and flopped down on the bed. The room was quiet with Chantel gone. The last test was being administered on a one on one basis over the course of the entire day. The groups that had already shown their specializations were going first, as usual, in order of highest rank to lowest. Chantel's test had been early that morning after she'd proven how badass her fire-starter skills were and landed the top slot in her new troupe. Jessie was going dead last.

Her two point lead had dwindled rapidly as the other novices began to either find their powers or give up. It seemed like each day was just a reminder that she was out of her league. She didn't need them, she tried to remind herself. She'd done just fine on her own before. She was dwelling on the negative more than she should. She needed to get over it and move on.

She'd already spent the day in solitude warring with herself over the pros and cons of just giving up. In the end, she was too stubborn not to see it through. At least then, if she did wash out, she wouldn't be haunted by the constant what ifs.

The silence of the room had only been broken once, when a member of the staff had come to collect Chantel's belongings to be moved to her new housing assignment. When she'd asked where Chantel was, the guy had just shrugged and loaded her luggage onto one of the trolleys left over from when the building had been a resort. A little hurt that her friend wouldn't come back and tell her how it was or what she was supposed to do, Jessie had just shaken her head.

Maybe it was better that way. Chantel had been the first real friend she could remember having. The idea of having to say goodbye in person hurt too much. Chantel had found her people in the novices and other students. She'd spread her wings flawlessly and was establishing a healthy amount of friendships on her own. She'd tried to include Jessie, but the lack of sleep had made it next to impossible to keep up.

Chantel would be alright with one less person to hang out with, and to Jessie that was what was important. Her shit was trivial as long as the people she cared about were happy and healthy. Unable to sit still anymore, Jessie left the room with her backpack over her shoulder. Jacob and the others had tried to convince her to stay a while if the worst happened, but that wasn't her plan. After the final test results were posted and troupes were finalized, there was going to be a big party in the main dining hall to celebrate the beginning of a new year.

That was the last place she wanted to be. She'd already checked to see if there was anyone heading in to Denver later that night. Finding nothing, she'd bribed one of the kitchen staff to drive her if she washed out with the last of the cash Zack had given her. Almost unconsciously, she felt her back pocket for the new card Bernal had sent to her room the day before with her name on it.

She knew she should give it back to him if she left, but beggars couldn't be choosers and she needed money to survive. He'd probably cancel it shortly after she'd left anyway, but if she was lucky he'd give her a few days before he did.

Knowing she still had a couple of hours to kill before her last test, she wandered the building aimlessly. She soaked in the beauty of the place, memorizing the rustic splendor mixed with high luxury and the subtle clunk of her heels on the marble floors. She'd probably never get to live so comfortably again, but at least she'd have the memory.

"Out of the way," a harried voice boomed as an EMT sprinted past her on her way to the test. She stepped to the side and flattened herself as best she could against the wall as two more followed, pushing an empty gurney.

"What the hell?" she whispered to herself. Unable to resist, she jogged down the hall after them to see what caused the commotion.

They stopped outside the dark room Jacob had prevented her from seeing on their tour and rushed inside with the gurney. She slowed her pace to a walk as she came closer and stayed against the wall in case someone else came blasting through. A girl's pained groans and whimpers came floating out of the room making her heart thump.

"She's stable," the EMT that had ordered her to move said. "Let's get her to her room so she can rest."

"She's one of mine," Ann said solemnly inside.

A minute later, one of the girls from Jessie's group was wheeled out on the gurney with an EMT on either side while the other pushed. She was as white as the sheet they'd covered her with and drenched in sweat. She twisted painfully back and forth as they rolled her past Jessie, and she felt her stomach wrench. What the fuck had happened to her?

"I don't think I can watch this anymore," Lena said. Nauseated horror twisted her voice and Jessie could hear her tears. "Why do you have to be so hard with them?"

"It's just how it is," she heard Luke say. He sounded out of breath and exhausted. She heard water splash lightly against metal, followed by someone breathing out heavily. "And I'm taking it easy on them compared to my test."

"Why are we even doing this test?" Ann snapped. "Everyone has already been placed."

"Not everyone," Luke said and she knew he meant her. She bit her lip and leaned closer to the open door to peer inside as best as she could without being seen. The windowless room was painted solid black and lit by rows of tall beige tapers, dripping wax as they burned at varying heights. In the corner of the room there was a small silver pot that was leaking smoke. It smelled like Dragon's Blood incense.

She knew Luke, Ann, and Lena were in the room by their voices, but she couldn't see them. She could, however, see Jacob standing with his arms crossed over his chest.

"One," he said. "That has all but made up her mind that she is going to fail. I'll admit, she has the potential to be a Mancer, I can feel it in her stronger than any of the other novices, but she's holding herself back."

"Maybe we could just give her a pass and let her stay on as my aid or something," Theo suggested, making her frown. "Maybe she's just not ready. If she stays, maybe she could pick up a few tricks and someday she'll be a Terramancer."

"She's not yours," Luke said with a growl. The possessive tone he used made Jessie grind her teeth.

"Back off, Lucifer," Jacob said with the heavy authority of being the senior Master. "He's just trying to help."

"She doesn't need his help," Luke whispered menacingly.

"She doesn't need anyone's," Jessie said as she stepped into the doorframe. She crossed her arms and stood with her feet shoulder width apart, trying to make herself seem larger than she really was. "I'm a big girl. I can take care of myself."

"Jessie," Lena said regretfully. "Please, don't be offended. We just care about you, that's all."

"I'm not offended," she said. "I'm just not a charity case. And," she looked at each of the Masters in turn, pegging them with a hard stare, "I don't need your pity or your protection." Jacob dropped his head with a sigh of defeat as the others at least had the grace to look chastened. Except Luke who had a smug smirk on his lips as he looked at her appreciatively. "Especially yours," she said to him.

That got rid of the smile on his face.

"Now, are we going to do this?" she asked. "Or have you all just written me off as a failure?"

"You're the one who's already packed," Luke pointed out harshly, his usual thorny bravado returning.

"Hope for the best and prepare for the worst," she said with a shrug. "I haven't given up, but I do have a backup plan. I always do."

"You don't have to do this test," Theo said, still trying to protect her from whatever was to come.

"Yes, she does," Luke said with a snarl.

"Yes, I do," Jessie said at the same time calmly.

They looked at each other briefly before Luke turned away and went back to the steel bowl in the center on the far wall. He put his hands on either side of the basin. He hung his head for a moment before using his hands to scoop water up and scrub his face. The sweat soaking his grey shirt seemed out of place in the coolness of the room. She looked around for the source of the AC, but only confirmed there were no vents in the room at all. The room was just a concrete box with a steel door.

"Come in, Jessie," Jacob said, "and close the door."

She did as instructed and Ann came over to take her backpack. Theo joined them by the door and threw the heavy lock, trapping them in together. Fear crept into her mind, kicking off a cacophony of noise as the voices started in on their "pep talks." The reasonable voice coached her to breathe and relax as the malignant voice started filling her brain with all the different tortures Luke had in store for her, cackling as Jessie tried to block them out.

"Are you alright?" Lena asked as she reached out and touched her shoulder.

"I'm fine," she said harsher than she meant to as Lena's concern and fear rampaged through her, adding fuel to the chaos. She shrugged off the touch and shivered as the feelings started to ebb away. "I'm fine," she said in a calmer voice. "Let's just get this over with."

Jacob moved her to the center of the room, into a white ritual circle painted on the floor, and stepped away. The Masters gathered near the door, making themselves as inconspicuous as possible as Luke turned around to face her slowly. He eyes roamed her body, sizing her up as he started to pace around her.

"You're different today," he said, but he sounded curious.

"How so?" she asked as she turned to follow him with her eyes. She didn't feel any different.

"More alert," he said quietly. "Less controlled."

"I haven't taken my medication since yesterday," she said.

He stopped in front of her with his back to the steel bowl and tilted his head, understanding dawning in his eyes.

"The voices keeping you awake at night?" he asked with a smirk and her heart sank.

"How did you know?" she whispered. She looked over her shoulder at the Masters and saw them all stand up straighter.

"Why didn't you tell anyone?" he asked, bringing her attention back to him.

Becausewhathappensinourheadisnoone'sfuckingbusiness.

Because they would have thought we were broken.

"Because I didn't," she said.

"You know, every story has three sides," Luke said as he stepped into the circle, forcing her to crane her neck to see his face. "His side. Her side. And, the truth."

"So?"

"So, the Spirare hear it all, whether they want to or not."

"What's your point, Luke?" she asked. He was lording his information over her and had been since he'd first mentioned his specialization. Every time she'd asked him, he'd just stared her down until she got frustrated and walked away.

"Spirare are the children of the angels," he said and she frowned.

"My father was human," she said. "He was a medic in the Army before he died."

He shook his head.

"He may not be alive, but he wasn't human," he said. "Spirare are the first generation. The other Mancer troupes began with the Spirare's children and so on. But, because we are born to an angel and a human, we are the Mancers closest to the Primal Source. Where the others need a physical element to channel the power, Spirare draw directly from it. Being Spirare means a lifetime trapped by the power, even if you were to leave now and run away, you'd never escape it. Not even death is an option for relief."

Jessie breathed deeply to steady her nerves and closed her eyes, letting his words sink in. "You mean I can't die?"

"No," he said. "I mean you can't die naturally or by suicide. Suicide is too selfish and nature doesn't want us. How you are now is how you'll be millennia from now. Benes from the fathers. But, there's a catch."

"There always is," she said to herself, rolling her eyes.

"Spirare are fighters," he continued as if she hadn't spoken. "Survivors, by design. We were bred to be the warriors the angels couldn't be on their own. We are the foot soldiers of our fathers. Think about it. When you see pain inflicted unjustly, a wrong going uncorrected, what do you do?"

"I fix it," she said.

"Not just try?" he asked smugly.

"Failure isn't an option," she said. It wasn't. Not if someone was in danger needlessly. Not if she could help it.

"That's what I thought," he said with a smile. He looked up at the Masters with the expressional equivalent of a fully extended middle finger and kept talking. "Are you ready?"

Jessie looked behind her and saw the Masters leaning forward slightly, completely absorbed in their exchange. None of them spoke or moved, so she looked back at Luke and nodded.

"This might hurt," he said bluntly.

"No apologizes?" she asked.

"No need," he said and his smile turned to one of pride. "You're a big girl. You can handle it."

She looked at him curiously as he reached for her hands and brought them up between them with his fingers wrapped around her palms. His hands were warm and dry, despite the sweat still clinging to his shirt, and they had a pleasantly rough texture. As their skin made contact, she felt the electricity shimmy through her again. But he didn't pull away.

She closed her eyes again as warmth spread through her and the room around them dropped away, leaving them suspended in a pocket of pearlescent black space. The effect he had was dizzying as she felt her muscles relax and her bones get soggy. In her mind, the voices started to scream, quietly at first, then growing louder and louder until they sounded like they were on the outside screaming in.

Then suddenly, it stopped. She felt hollow in her own skin as she opened her eyes and looked up at Luke. But he wasn't alone anymore.

Two women stood to either side of him, staring at her. They were her height, and they had her face, but she'd never seen them before. The one that stood to his left cocked her head at an unnatural angle, her bright green eyes blazing with sadistic malice and insanity. Her waist length black hair was matted and her fingers twitched at her sides like she was resisting the urge to tear at her scalp.

The other stood serenely, smiling as her blue eyes sparkled with quiet pride. Her square face was pale and dewy with a healthy glow in her defined cheekbones. She was gorgeous, but the dark circles under her eyes made her look exhausted.

"Hello," she said timidly to the blue eyed girl.

Her smile brightened and she nodded in greeting, but didn't say a word. Jessie looked back up into Luke's face intending to ask him what was going on, but it was twisted in agony.

"Luke?" she asked in growing alarm. "What's wrong?"

"He's protecting us," the blue eyed girl said softly. She was the reasonable voice personified. "He's afraid the Primal Source would tear us apart if he didn't."

"He's fucking burning, you moron," the green eyed girl hissed. "He's burning himself up because of you."

"No," Jessie said. "What do I have to do?" she asked the blue eyed girl.

"He's drawing the excess power into himself," she said calmly.

Her apathy was starting to get on Jessie's nerves. "If you want to save him, you have to take it from him."

"This is where they failed," the green eyed girl laughed as she gave into the urge to grip her hair tightly. "This is where they all failed. And, you'll fail, too. You worthless piece of shit. You always fail. You're poison," she spat and then started to cackle and shriek.

"You can do it," the blue eyed girl said, ignoring her twin. "Just draw it out."

Luke started to grip her hands tighter, squeezing her palms until she felt like her bones would break. She took a deep breath and trusted her instincts. With a herculean effort, she shifted one hand out of his grip and touched his face.

His eyes snapped open and he stared at her, concern and fear warring with his pain.

"It's ok," she told him, and she meant it. "Trust me."

"It's too much," he said as he began to shake.

"You're pulling in more energy than the others," the blue eyed girl smiled. "He only gave them a taste of the energy, and it almost killed them."

"Kill them," the green eyed girl snapped. "Kill them all."

"He's afraid he won't be able to regulate it with you."

Instantly, she knew what she needed to do. He was hurting himself to protect her. If their roles had been reversed she would have done the same if she knew she could survive. He was more experienced than her. But, she was stronger than she looked. She stepped closer to him, closing the distance between their bodies and wrapped her arm around his waist.

She felt with the deepest part of her for the energy he was holding back. Her breath caught as the tugging she'd felt when they first met came back like a punch to her chest, pulsing with power as the energy started to flow into her. It was slow at first, feeling its way through her like a living thing. Seeming to approve of what it found, it poured into the hollow spaces left behind by the voices until she felt like her skin would burst.

Her vision dimmed as Luke's hand relaxed its grip. She felt his strong arm wrap around her, holding her close as she took it in, forcing herself to contain it. Her nails dug into the small of his back as her fingers twisted into the fabric of his shirt. Tears sprang to her eyes, but she grit her teeth and forced them down. She could feel a shriek building in her throat as the torrent continued and Luke whispered words of comfort into her hair.

"It's alright, focul iadului," he said, curling his big body around hers so that his lips brushed her ear. "You can do this."

She wanted to ask what he wanted her to do, but she was afraid if she opened her mouth she'd lose control. She couldn't lose control again. Images of the community center flickered behind her eye lids. It was a slaughter. She'd flipped the switch on the people inside, stripping them of their morals and decency only to replace it with a blood lust so strong they'd ripped each other limb from limb just to watch the carnage flow.

"You can control it," he whispered and rested his temple against hers. "I know you can." She felt his lips brush her cheek as his calm certainty began to temper the edge of the energy's gnawing teeth.

Breathing rapidly, she steeled her nerves and pushed the energy out and away from Luke. The sudden emptiness inside her stole her breath as the power exploded from between her shoulder blades and curled around them. Luke's impressed chuckle helped her relax as she started to sag in his arms.

"Look, focul iadului," he said, his awed voice quiet.

Slowly, she opened her eyes and looked around. The room and the candles were back where they had been. Hovering around them and closing them off from the Masters, were large translucent wings of pearlescent black. She was speechless.

Carefully, she reclaimed her weight from Luke's embrace and

stepped away from him. She had to be sure it was her creating them, otherwise she wouldn't believe it. Her heart thudded in her chest as they came with her and flexed as she willed them to. She looked up at Luke with unabashed pride that matched his as she folded them down. "Piece of cake," she said as they started to retreat and dissolve into her back.

Those were her last words before the world tilted and the floor rushed up to say hello.

Chapter 11

Jessie woke up in the center of a toasted marshmallow, surrounded by the scent of pure male and Irish Spring. She would have enjoyed the warmth and comfort, had she not wanted to die. She felt like she had gone on a weeklong drinking binge. After catching the plague. And being hit by a car. Everything fucking hurt.

"How are you feeling?" Luke's quiet voice asked beside her. She opened her eyes and immediately regretted it as the soft light from the lamp across the room pierced her optic nerve.

"Ow," she said. It was the only word she had enough sense to form.

"I know," he said. "The kind of energy you pulled in would have shredded a lesser Mancer." A cool, wet cloth touched her forehead and she groaned in gratitude. "I'm proud of you."

She didn't want to admit how much that meant to her. She was still pissed at him for being an asshole to her all week. She wanted to smack him for leaving her in the lurch and keeping secrets. She wanted to scream at him for not giving her a heads up on what to expect during his test. She wanted to jump on him and make sure he was ok after trying to protect her. But, all she could manage was a weak, "Dick."

He chuckled and she heard the sound of water sloshing somewhere nearby as he rewetted the cloth and returned it to her forehead. "So vicious for someone who can't even open their eyes," he said with a light-hearted challenge in his voice. She took a deep breath and turned her head towards the sound of his voice. She gave the whole open-your-eyes bit another go. She managed a pained squint with one eye.

The first thing she noticed was that he'd changed his sweaty shirt for a white one and his hair was wet. The second was his expression. He was grinning like an idiot. She groaned at him and tried to sit up, but her muscles said fuck-that and gave out. She dropped like a stone back into the soft mattress with a whump and whimpered. "I don't think so, focul iadului," he said and replaced the wet cloth with his fingertips. "You took a beating today and I want you to rest."

"Bossy," she whispered.

"You're part of my troupe now," he said and she could hear the stupid smile in his voice. "Get used to it."

"Never," she said and tried to open her eyes again. It was easier that time and warmth was spreading through her from his touch. "Are you healing me?"

"Not consciously," he said and moved his fingers away from her skin.

The warmth faded almost instantly, and the sudden return of pain made her nauseous. She closed her eyes again and rolled away to curl up in the fetal position as the waves lumbered through her. She felt the mattress dip beside her and Luke's giant arm slipped around her belly. As presumptuous as it was for him to assume that was ok, she was thankful for his help. She wrapped herself around his arm as best as she could and breathed deep as the warmth returned to sooth her.

"Where am I?" she asked once the worst had passed.

"My room," he said quietly above her head. Through their contact she could feel him getting nervous as he waited for her to respond.

"Why?" she asked.

"You and I are the only active Spirare at MERCE," he said. "I didn't have any other rooms prepped." He was kicking himself internally at the lack of foresight. "I'm sorry."

"It's ok," she said. She pushed reassurance through to him and he relaxed. "I can sleep on the floor from now on."

"No," he said a little more sternly than she would have liked. She was afraid he'd say she had to sleep in his room with him, but he followed it up with, "I'll take the couch."

"It's ok," she said as she released her hold on his arm and rolled over to face him. He lifted his arm away from her and mirrored her position with his hands folded under his head. "I've slept in worse places," she said and used her thumb to smooth the crease between his eyebrows.

"I know," he whispered and winced. She frowned at him and the crease returned. "I want to tell you something, but I don't know how," he said after a few heartbeats of silence.

"Just tell me," she said. It wasn't that hard.

His frown deepened as he looked at her and worry started to tease the edge of her mind. She almost jerked away when he touched her cheek carefully, but the feeling he was pushing through to her made her hesitate. There was pain there, and regret. There was also the bone deep conviction that she was going to hate him until time ceased to exist. She braced herself as a memory floated to the surface of his emotions.

He was standing on the corner of a small street. There was more open, dry grassland than businesses. But he wasn't there for the scenery.

Two hundred yards away from his position, blue and red lights flashed in front of a smoldering pile of ash. Smoke still blanketed the area, but he could see well enough. A dozen officers in tan uniforms surrounded a suspect with their guns drawn. The suspect was screaming and clawing at her scalp. She was begging for them to pull the trigger. She wanted to die.

He'd felt her power from miles away and come to investigate. He'd watched her as she watched the community center burn. He'd thought she was a Pyromancer, but he couldn't be sure. She wasn't his assignment there, but something wouldn't let him leave. When the Troopers had finally subdued her, she was sobbing that someone was stolen from her.

He'd called Bernal that same night and told him he'd found a Mancer that needed help. Her face was on the local news flickering on the ancient TV set in his shitty motel room and he'd watched the whole story play out. Her name was Jessica Mead. She was a local lunatic that the town had feared since she was a child according to eyewitnesses. They'd accused her of killing her son, Daniel, but no evidence of the crime had been found. She'd started screaming to anyone who would listen that a local motorcycle club had been responsible for her son's disappearance, but again, no evidence was found.

The community center had been their last place to party after a run. The building had been abandoned some time before, and they'd been using it illegally after their property had burned. Just one of many arson cases within the past 72 hours that had yet to be solved. She was just another Pyromancer that had been driven insane by the energy she didn't understand and grief had made her snap.

But he hadn't been able to leave it alone and let Bernal deal with the Mancer. He'd visited her family's home and found a woman about her age named Teresa who'd tried to slam the door of their trailer in his face, but he'd gotten into her head before she could. He'd replayed the day she and her mother had driven the Pyromancer out of her home with nothing more than a backpack full of clothes and wanted to kill them on principle alone. They'd believed the Pyromancer was responsible for the boy's death, too, and they couldn't handle her constant insistence that he was alive. Teresa was the boy's birth mother, but even in her memory she couldn't bring herself to think of him as her son. She'd lost that privilege and she hated her sister for taking it away.

He'd pushed his way in and caught the feel of the Pyromancer's energy as best he could before following her footsteps. She'd tracked someone from the park where the boy was taken. It was faint, but he knew something was driving her. She had been the one who burned down eight properties in three days. When he came to the last one, the smoldering skeleton of a barn, he'd followed her steps to a small thicket of thin trees.

That was where he found the grave. It was smaller than his torso and had been dug by hand. Her grief still flavored the air and earth from her sobs as she'd clawed at the dirt to dig it. Sitting on the small mound of dirt was a handful of plastic dinosaurs that were damaged and faded from play. He picked up the tyrannosaurus that had been worn smooth on the sides. It had been her son's favorite and took it everywhere with him. Luke had to breathe deep as her pain rushed through him and he returned the toy. He'd run his fingers through the loose earth and found the end of a charred bone.

It was all that was left of the boy.

When Luke released his grip on her mind, Jessie scrambled back and off the mattress. It was a lie. Daniel was alive. He had to be alive. He was lying to her, torturing her.

Liketheytorturedhim.

"No," she said with a gasp and grabbed the sides of her head as she remembered what had driven her mad that day. She'd found where they had taken him. She'd found the hollowed out remains of the barn still glowing with embers. They'd taken Daniel. They'd locked him up in cage and starved him. They'd taunted him as he cried. Then they'd burned him when their deal with the devil went south. "No," she said through gritted teeth. It wasn't true. "Not again."

She bolted. She saw her backpack on a chair by the door and snatched it up as she fled. She found the front door to the apartment and clawed it open as Luke's thundering footfalls chased after her. In the hall, she had no idea what floor she was on, but there were only three other doors aside from the elevator. One across the way. One next to her. And another marked stairs.

"Jessie," he called. "Please, let me explain."

She slammed through the door marked stairs so fast she almost lost her footing and fell. She practically jumped down each flight of steps deeper and deeper down. It was the only way she could go. She broke through the door at the bottom and barely paused. She needed to get away. She couldn't stay there. There were too many lies.

They'retryingtotakehimawayagain.

He's already lost.

She ground her teeth together so tight she thought her jaw would snap as she ran for the main dining room. She'd bribed one of the kitchen staff to drive her to Denver before the test. She needed to find him. The novice party. He had to be there. Her skin was crawling with the need to get away. She could feel Luke's power following her. She wasn't sure how, but she knew it was him.

He'stryingtotakehimawayagain.

He's already gone.

"Gorgeous!" Chantel called out over the music playing over the speakers lining the dining hall. "You stayed!"

Chantel bounded up to Jessie and hugged her so tightly it was all Jessie could do to keep from shoving her away. As it was, she practically knocked her over in an effort to free herself. "I'm leaving."

"What?" Chantel asked with a frown. "But, Theo said you didn't have to leave if you washed out. Hey, are you alright?"

"No," she said flatly as she continued to search for the staff member she needed. She knew she would miss Chantel's bubbly nature, but at that moment she couldn't give a shit. Luke appeared in the entrance to the dining hall, craning his neck as he searched for her.

"What does that psychopath want?" Chantel said with groan. "They should lock him up for what he did to us today. No one can handle that much energy head on." Jessie grabbed Chantel by her sleeve and dragged her through the back door as she continued to prattle on. "It was like having my brain sucked out through my eyeballs while being flayed by a shard of salt rock," Chantel said, oblivious to the fact that her voice was making Jessie's head throb. "What was the point in that?"

"He was testing for Spirare," Jessie said as she shoved Chantel beside the floor to ceiling windows and used the solid wall beside it to hide.

"Spirare are extinct," Chantel said flippantly. "They have been for centuries."

"He is one," Jessie said and grabbed Chantel by the sides of her face to get her attention. "I need you to distract him."

"What?"

"Just keep him inside. I have to get out of here and I can't while he's on my tail," Jessie told her, pressing urgency into her until she nodded.

She couldn't wait for the staff member. Luke was a Tracker and she was on his turf. He'd find her in seconds if she stuck around. The voices were still taunting her, screaming and sobbing inside her head, but the adrenaline was helping her focus.

"Jessie, what's going on?" Chantel asked as she released her and stepped away, surveying the landscape for the fastest route to the garages. She could hotwire a car and drive herself to Denver. She'd ditch it there and hitchhike back to Rankine.

"I just have to go," she said and started to take off, but Chantel grabbed her hand.

"Talk to me," she begged.

"Let me go!"

Her tenuous hold on her sanity snapped at the feeling of being trapped and she bared her teeth at Chantel. Her friend dropped her hand like a venomous snake and backed away with stark terror in her eyes. Her fear fueled the fire as she fought the urge to reach into her friend's mind and share her pain. She turned on her heel and sprinted away towards the woods.

She was halfway across the field when she heard the slow steady drum of giant wings buffeting the air behind her. She picked up her speed but it continued to gain more ground, closing the gap faster than her legs could move.

Luke soared over her head and landed in front of her, stretching his translucent wings out fifteen feet to either side and boxing her in as she headed straight for him. She dropped to the ground and slid to the side to stop before he could touch her. His hand snapped out as she scrambled to her feet, but she dodged him with a hiss.

"You can't run anymore, Jessica," he said. "You have to face the truth. Your son is dead. There's nothing you can do to change that."

"You lie," she said with a growl. "You're just trying to stop me."

"From what?" he snapped, moving to the side to cut her off as she tried to get around him. "Chasing a ghost for the rest of your life? From letting others use your grief against you? I'm trying to protect you."

"Fuck you," she spat and bolted in the other direction, back towards the school. Students had begun to gather outside the doors, bottlenecking the exit. She started to veer to the side, but Luke landed in front of her again.

She couldn't flee. So she attacked. She used her momentum to catch him low and throw him off balance. He wrapped his arm around her as he fell, pulling her with him to the ground, but the impact shook his hold enough for her to escape. She tried to leap over him, but his hand snapped out and grabbed her ankle.

She turned like a wild animal and sank her teeth into his bicep. Blood rushed into her mouth as she felt his flesh give and he grunted in pain. He slammed the heel of his free hand into the side of her head but she only bit harder and locked her jaw. Baring his teeth, he grabbed her by her braid and wrenched her head back.

Her hold slipped as he tore the skin further and he tossed her to the side by her hair. Stars exploded behind her eyes as her skull bounced off the ground. Before she could catch her breath, he was on her, pinning her to the ground by the shoulders and straddling her hips to keep her from flipping. She tossed and kicked, but it was like trying to move a mountain.

Slowly, warmth and calm reason shoved its way into her. She fought it, screeching in pain as he forced her to feel everything she had been denying. He ripped the grief she'd kept at bay out of the darkest depths of her soul and slammed it in her face. He wasn't going to let her lie to herself anymore.

"It's cruel," he'd yelled at Bernal in his office. His memory of that day mingled with the memory of the day she'd found Daniel's remains. "Dangling something like that in front of someone is wrong."

"It's the only thing that's keeping her here," Bernal had said more calmly.

"So, she'll leave. Good riddance! She doesn't need your bullshit promises and false hope."

"You're so quick to let her go when it was you who brought her to my attention? You may not see it, but you've already started to bond. You know that once the bond forms, Spirare need each other to survive. That's why you work best in pairs," Bernal had reminded him as he'd gestured for Luke to calm down.

"Spirare don't need anyone! We don't *need* anything from anyone! No, I will not calm down."

"Lucifer, please."

"Fuck you, Bernie. And fuck your bonding bullshit."

The memory faded as Jessie started to calm down, her rage giving way to the sting of betrayal. Bernal had known. He'd known that Daniel was gone. That there was no getting him back. But, he'd still used it to manipulate her into coming to MERCE. "Why?" she asked as she fought the sob gathering in her throat.

"I don't know," he said quietly. "I thought I could trust him until he told me the deal he'd made you. I'm sorry, Jessie."

His sympathy pushed through to her and she couldn't fight it anymore. Her heart and soul tore themselves apart as she realized he hadn't lied to her. She felt scraped hollow on the inside as he let her go. Her sobs rocked through her, devastating everything she had in its path. He let her cry, curling in on herself, and shielded them from view with his wings.

She didn't know how long it took for her to start to breathe again. Hours. Days. Centuries. But, when exhaustion crashed through her, he gathered her up and lifted them from the ground in a single, fluid motion. He landed them on the balcony that stretched across the back side of the sixth floor and recalled his wings. The energy dissolved and settled on his skin where it was absorbed into the grey latticework.

He cradled her with one arm as he slid the glass door open and pushed through the curtains into his bedroom. When he settled her back onto the mattress, she knew she'd been defeated. She couldn't leave. Even if she still wanted to, she had nowhere to go. She had nothing left to keep her going. Daniel was gone. And so was her heart.

Luke didn't leave her that night. She was in too much agony to care as he tucked her under the blankets, but as he started to turn away, she grabbed his hand. Silently, he nodded and slid in next to her. His warmth started to spread over her as he gathered her into his arms against his chest. He was trying to heal her pain.

He tucked her head under his chin and breathed deeply as she felt him start to leech her grief out of her and into himself. "Sleep, inimioara," he whispered as his other hand smoothed her hair. She wasn't sure she could, but, between the soothing strokes of his hand and the comfort he was feeding to her through his touch, exhaustion won.

Chapter 12

The next morning, she opened her swollen eyes to a wall of white and a soft puffing sound. She was stiff and sore, but she shifted her head back to find Luke fast asleep and snoring lightly. The events that had lead them there, wrapped up in each other slammed into her, but the raw agony she'd felt had started to ebb to a dull roar.

She started to move and Luke inhaled deeply as he started to wake up, too. He blinked and stared at her for a minute as his ruby eyes focused slowly. When it seemed to sink in that what he was seeing was real, he forced his eyes to open wide before settling them on her with his full attention. "How are you feeling?"

"It still hurts," she admitted as treacherous tears sprang to her eyes at having to say it out loud.

"It always will, inimioara," he whispered and touched her cheek. "But, it will get easier. I promise."

"Thank you," she whispered and pressed her cheek into his hand so he could feel her sincerity. "I'm sorry I bit you," she said as she touched the angry welt marring his skin with the shape of her teeth. Dried blood stained his sleeve and chest, but the wound had already healed over. She doubted it would even leave a scar.

"I called you hellfire for a reason," he said with a lazy shrug. "I knew when I went after you that you were going to fight. I would have been disappointed if you didn't."

"It sounded like you were saying 'fuck you, ya dually,'" she admitted.

"What's a dually?" he asked with an eyebrow raised.

"No clue. I thought you insulted me the first time you said it."

"I meant it as a compliment," he said.

"What language is that?" she asked. Talking about stupid shit was helping her take her mind off of losing Daniel. She'd never forget him completely, but she owed it to herself to at least try and move on.

"Romanian," he said. "I grew up in a village in the foothills of the Carpathians. Bernal brought me here when I was fifteen."

"How long have you been here?"

"Eleven years. I've got nowhere else to go," he said quietly as he lifted her tattered braid from the mattress and started to fidget with the end. "From what I saw of your hometown, I think you can relate to why I left. The people in my village called me 'diavol' when I was growing up. It means devil," he explained when he saw the question in her eyes.

"Why do they hate us?" she asked. It was the first time she'd asked it out loud, but it was a question that had haunted her entire life.

"Mundane people can feel our energy and it scares them. That's partly why we are so rare. The angels don't breed often. Even when they do, a Spirare child is not guaranteed," he said quietly. "You have a sister right?"

"My twin," she said. "But, she's not like me."

"That just means she couldn't handle the power of the Primal Source in utero," he said with a shrug. "If the fetus can't handle the power, the potential is lost and the child is mundane. You were strong enough to handle it."

"I don't think she's strong enough to handle a lot of things,"

Jessie whispered as she thought of how easily Teresa had given up taking care of their mother and Daniel. She'd said she couldn't handle dealing with them constantly.

"As long as I've been here, you're one of only a handful of Spirare that I've met. Damn near all of us are damaged," he said and she could see the sorrow in his eyes. "As much as I hate him for hurting you the way he did, I'm grateful to Bernal for bringing you here."

"I don't know if I'll ever go that far," she admitted. "But, I am thankful that you found me. And, thank you for forcing me to stop lying to myself."

"I would have wanted you to do the same to me," he said. "Do you still want to leave?" he asked as he focused on her braid again.

"If I did, would you let me?"

"I wouldn't want to," he admitted, still not looking her in the eyes. "But, if that's what you truly want, I would."

She stared at him as he stared at the ends of her hair and reached out to touch his cheek. He fought the intrusion into his head at first, but only for a moment before letting her in. She wasn't doing it out of spite or malicious intent, but she had to know. Carefully, she chased his fear to the surface. He was afraid of being alone. She understood. More than she wanted to.

Without pausing to ask herself why, she shifted her position cautiously and rested her head on his chest. When she wrapped her arm over his torso and threw her leg over his thigh, he froze. He wasn't used to being accepted. Then again, neither was she. He timidly put his arms around her. When she didn't pull away or let go, he squeezed her to him tightly and exhaled in relief.

"Ok," she said as she lifted her head and put her chin between his pecs. He looked down at her in question. "Enough of this mushy gushy bullshit. I need a shower and coffee. Not sure if that's the right order."

He laughed and a rare, genuine smile broke out across his face.

"You shower. I'll make coffee."

"Good man," she smiled and climbed over him, making sure to elbow him in the abs as she did. He groaned and chuckled as she retrieved her backpack from where he'd dropped it the night before. "Where's the bathroom?"

He pointed to the door beside the bed as he sat up and stretched. She opened it and found a walk-in closet as big as her bedroom in the trailer in Rankine. There weren't many clothes hanging up, but the space was enough to make her pause. He came up behind her and pushed past to the door at the back. He flicked on a light and stood to the side so she could enter.

And she thought the closet was huge. He had a tub large enough for him to lay down in with a steam shower next it. Along the wall were acres of black marble counter space with two steel skins sunken into it and a mirror that stretched the entire length. Even the toilet looked expensive. "Holy shit."

He chuckled. "It takes some getting used to. I still don't think I have. Your room mirrors the layout of mine, by the way. So, don't worry about losing out."

"Serving me an eviction notice already?" she asked as she set her backpack down next to his antique shaving kit, complete with ivory handled straight razor.

"Not yet," he shrugged. "But, I ordered a bed yesterday after your test, so you should be in your own space by the end of the week."

"You can have it," she smiled and he tilted his head in question. "I plan on stealing yours."

He smirked. "It's a package deal."

"We'll see," she said as she picked up his straight razor and turned it between her palms. "I'll fight you for it. I won't even hold back this time."

He shook his head and stared at her. He was trying to glare, but his smirk stayed in place. "Neither will I."

Chapter 13

Jessie stepped out of the steam shower feeling better than she had in a long time. She wasn't sure if it was because of Luke's subconscious healing while they slept or if it was because she'd finally stopped lying to herself. But, she felt more... balanced. Depression still hovered at the edges, but she knew if she kept moving it would help.

She needed to find a new purpose to keep her going. If what Luke had said during her testing was right, if she gave in and shut down it would mean an eternity of suffering. Where part of her felt that was what she deserved, she was too much of a survivor to give in without a fight. With a deep breath, she blocked the temptation of sorrow out and took her first steps towards recovery.

She'd finished her routine of teeth-brushed-hair-braided and turned to leave when something caught her eye in the mirror. Squinting through the steamy haze still clinging to the glass, she leaned in close and stared at her shoulder.

"The fuck?" she whispered as she wiped the glass clear. There was a red line curling over her skin on both shoulders. It looked like a rash. "Luke!"

She heard his footfalls thundering towards her from another room not far away. He burst through the door and his head swiveled around, surveying the room. Finding nothing his eyes settled on her and flared before he slammed them shut and clapped a hand over them. "Damn it, woman, I thought you were hurt."

"I think I have a rash," she explained and he dropped his head with a groan.

"I'm not a doctor," he said. "If you have a rash, go to the infirmary."

"I don't need you to treat it, jackass. I can't see it very well. I need your help," she said.

"To do what?" he asked warily.

"Describe it to me," she told him and turned her back to him before dropping the backside of the towel below her shoulders. "Please, Luke? Daniel used to get rashes all the time. If I know what kind I'm dealing with I can treat it myself."

With a martyred sigh, he dropped his hand and looked at her back. He frowned at first and then started to tug the towel farther down. She yelped as her grip started to slip and clutched the fabric to her chest. "Hey, hey!"

"Sorry," he said, but she didn't think he meant it as he moved her braid to the side and had her lean forward. "It's not a rash," he said finally.

"Then what the hell is it?" she asked. He took his index fingers and traced the edges as he pushed the image of what he was seeing into her head. "Wings?"

"Yep," he said with a smirk as they looked at each other in the mirror. "They must've started coming in last night. They're pretty. Not as big as mine, but still."

"Huh?" she asked as she turned to face him.

Instead of answering her, he peeled his shirt off over his head and turned around. She'd seen the energy absorb into the ink in his skin, but she'd never focused on the design close enough to realize it wasn't just latticework. From the tops of his shoulders to below his belt and wrapping around his biceps and forearms were painstakingly detailed feathered wings. The only bare skin he had left was a single space below his neck the size of her hand. "Wow," she said and rested her palm in the space as her eyes analyzed every detail.

"Every Spirare carry the mark of their kind," he said gruffly. He cleared his throat and stepped away from her touch to face her. "It comes from the first time we channel the energy of the Primal Source and then release it through us. You chose the form of wings just like I did."

"So, that means?"

"When they have fully developed, you'll be able to summon them at will, without having to draw in the level of power you did during testing," he said.

She bit her lip and stared at the designs on his skin, remembering what it'd felt like to be weightless in the air. She could do that? She smiled to herself and turned her back to the mirror. She tilted her head as she looked at the design but she couldn't see the whole thing. She let the towel slide a little lower without thinking and Luke cleared his throat uncomfortably.

"Sorry," she said and pulled the terrycloth back up.

"It's ok," he said, "but, unless you want me getting an eye-full I suggest you get dressed."

"Fair enough," she shrugged and followed him out.

He left the room to give her privacy and she dressed quickly after sneaking another peek at the design on her back. The wings may not have wrapped around her arms the way his did, but they took up her whole back, curling down the natural curve of her waist and over her hips.

She was curious if they would get darker or not. They seemed fine red, but the idea of looking like she had a perpetual rash wasn't appealing. Curiosity sated, she followed the scent of fresh coffee out into the hall. She was in the room on the end of a hall with six doors. The one directly next to Luke's was a mirror image that was barren of furniture. That must have been hers.

Two more rooms stood empty, but they didn't have windows or

bathrooms. The rhythmic sound of a keyboard clicking brought her attention away from the guest bathroom she'd found and into the last room on her left. She poked her head through the open door and stumbled. The walls were lined with shelves on three sides, including over the door. The shelves were packed with books. Before Daniel was born, she'd loved escaping into the pages of a decent fantasy novel, but she'd only had a few.

Her new roommate had to have been a hardcore bibliophile. He was sitting in an oversized leather office chair, leaning forward over an ergonomic keyboard. Front and center on his admiral's desk were three wide, flat monitors arranged in a slight curve. Beside him on a special stand that looked custom made was a Frankenstein of a computer tower, complete with novelty bolts on the sides and blinking green LEDs inside. "Holy nerd-alert, Batman," she said with a disbelieving shake of her head.

"Don't judge," he said without turning around. She stood next to his chair and watched the screens. He was typing, so fast her hands hurt just watching him, and clicking through his extended display. It looked like some kind of a report complete with topographical maps with virtual pins in them. The screen furthest to the left had a scrolling line of text in three colors; white, blue, and green.

The last line read was green, "Who's the girl?"

She titled her head when she read it and a new line popped up in blue. "She's cute, Luci. Definite keeper."

Green: Shit, we've been spotted.

Blue: I know right? *does sexy dance* You like what you see?

Green: Damn it, Gabby. Shut up.

Blue: Come over here and make me.

Green: I swear to the fathers, I will kick your ass.

Blue: Try it and I'll dick slap you.

"Luke?" she asked and he looked up at the screen. He shook his head and tapped a few keys to bring that screen to the front. Apparently, he was white.

Luke: Both of you, knock it off or I'll slap the shit out of you myself.

Blue: How about your new lady friend? I wouldn't mind being smacked around by her a little bit.

Green: Dude!

Luke: She bites.

Blue: Woo Hoo! My kind of woman.

Green: I can't take you anywhere.

Luke: I'm not sure you'd like it.

Blue: I would if she was naked. From the look of your arm, my man, she likes it rough. Am I right?

Luke groaned and threw the bloodied shirt he'd put on his desk over the monitor. She looked at him with an eyebrow raised. "I'm not sure if I should be flattered or insulted," she told him.

"Gabby is a decent guy, he's just," he paused, "off."

"Yeah, but who is he?"

"A friend," he said and reached back to touch her arm. "You'll meet him eventually. I apologize for it now."

"So what are you doing besides virtual babysitting?" she asked as she pulled his chair back and flopped down in his lap. She took shirt off the monitor, stole his mouse, and pulled up the maps he'd been pouring over.

"My job," he said with a groan. "Do you mind?"

"Nope," she said and continued to click through the pages. She didn't understand a damned word. "What the hell, man?"

"I take notes in my native language," he said as he stole the mouse back and closed the tab. "It's easier."

"For who?"

"Me," he said as he stood up, forcing her to do so, too. "They're my notes."

He didn't offer any further explanation as he led her out of his office. She wanted to keep prodding for information, but the sight of the apartment's main living space made her lose her train of thought.

It was an open, airy penthouse apartment large enough to comfortably fit the entire novice class if they packed them in together.

The main living space boasted maple floors, a big screen TV hanging over the working fireplace, and a chocolate brown, overstuffed leather couch big enough for Luke to stretch out on and still have space for her to sit comfortably. Beside the couch was a matching chair and ottoman with a small table next to it stacked with books. Looking at the titles on the comfortably worn spines, she couldn't help but smile. It looked like Luke had a weak spot for the Dresden Files.

Behind that was a wall of floor to ceiling windows leading out onto a wide balcony that overlooked the back of the property and gave her a breathtaking view of the mountains. There was even a small table with two chairs to sit and enjoy the scenery. She wanted to go out there and just stand in the breeze, but her curiosity got the better of her.

At the back of the space, there was a huge, gourmet kitchen kitted out in black quartz, deep mahogany, and stainless steel. There was a dining area in the same colors just in front of it, separated by a bar-top counter and sporting a heavy, antique dining table large enough to seat ten people.

She ran her hands over the elaborate scrolling design of one of the high-backed dining chairs and looked up at the vaulted ceiling in amazement. There had to have been some kind of mistake. There was no way she was supposed to be up there. The place even had its own laundry room, which meant she wouldn't have to battle for a washing machine with the other students when she wanted clean underwear.

"Are you sure this is just for us?" she asked as she joined Luke in the kitchen and took the oversized mug full of fresh coffee he held out for her.

"That was my response," he said with a chuckle and took a sip from his own mug. "But, it's just us up here."

"Who used to live here?" she asked as she put some sugar in her mug and stirred it. There was way too much room for just two people.

"Back in the day, the fathers would stay here to be closer to their children," he shrugged. "They stayed in the penthouses and their kids stayed downstairs with the other troupes."

"Why'd they stop?"

"They got bored with us," he said with a surprising amount of venom. "Can we change the subject?"

"You know, changing subjects during an uncomfortable conversation is a fetish of mine," she said using her mug to hide her grin. She was rapidly realizing that giving him a hard time was going to be her new favorite hobby. "What's yours?"

She stared at him as he opened his mouth and closed it again. Finally, he gave up, walked back into his office, and closed the door. Laughing, she took her mug out on the balcony to enjoy the breeze.

She'd been outside for about an hour when he walked out from his bedroom in a fresh shirt and jeans. When he spotted her, he marched down to where she was sitting with a sour expression.

"Deal with this," he said with a growl as he handed a cell phone to her. She looked at the screen in confusion and then lifted it to her ear.

"Hello?" she asked. Chantel's panicked voice screeched in her ear. She wasn't sure the girl was even speaking real words, but she thought she made out the words "where are you". "I'm home," she said and frowned up at Luke as he stood with his arms crossed over his chest and his face locked down tight. "I'm fine. What's wrong?"

"What's wrong? What's wrong! You tell me what's wrong. Last night you try to run away like you were being hunted. Then you get tackled by that Neolithic Big Bird and whisked away to God knows where. Then I try to call you, you don't answer! I had to steal Theo's phone just to get Mr. Personality's number. I thought you'd been kidnapped or something!"

"You thought I'd been kidnapped, so you called my kidnapper?" Jessie asked carefully. "You do understand the flaw in that logic, right?"

"Where the fuck are you!" she screamed and Jessie moved the phone away from her ear.

"I told you. I'm home," she said with a sigh and rubbed her forehead. She jumped when Luke's hand touched her shoulder and she looked up at him.

"You ok?" he whispered. She touched his fingers and pushed her reassurance through to him. He breathed heavily once and nodded before going back inside.

"And where exactly is that?" Chantel asked. She watched Luke retreat into the hall, presumably to go back to his office.

"With Luke," she said without thinking.

"With Luke?" Chantel asked in disbelief. "Where? In a cave in the middle of the woods? Is he torturing you? I swear to God I will turn his sorry ass into ash."

"Seriously, Chantel, I'm fine. I promise. Last night I," she choked on the words, telling her she was still raw. "I had a bit of a break down and I didn't handle it as well as I could have. I'm sorry if I scared you."

"*IF!*" she shrieked.

"I'm sorry I scared you," Jessie said. "As bad as it looked, Luke was actually the only one who could have gotten through to me last night. I owe him big time."

"You don't owe him shit," Chantel said and Jessie could picture her scowl.

"Yes, I do," Jessie said and meant it. He'd met her straight on without pause, even when she'd been trying to hurt him. If anyone else had tried, she would have killed them. "Look, if you want I can come and meet you somewhere so you can see for yourself that I'm in one piece."

"Ten minutes. Rec room," Chantel said.

"Twenty and the back lawn," she said. She needed to tell Chantel the truth, but she didn't want to be around a lot of people.

"Fine." She hung up before Jessie could say goodbye. With a sigh of defeat, she took her empty mug and went back inside. After she washed the mug and put it in the dryer next to the sink, she went to give Luke back his phone. "I've been summoned," she said by way of greeting.

"Want me to come with you?" he offered, but she knew he really didn't want to.

"It's just Chantel," she said with a shrug and then she paused. "You wouldn't happen to have a weapon I could bring, would you?"

He chuckled and shook his head. "Afraid not," he said. "I think my sword is a bit too big for you." She perked an eyebrow and waited for him to realize what he said. "You pervert."

"You said it," she said with a shrug and walked away.

"Keep your phone on," he called after her. "Preferably with the ringer on."

"I don't know how to work this thing," she admitted as she came back with her shoes on and her backpack over her shoulder. "I thought I turned the ringer on, but I never hear it."

He woke the phone up and tapped it with his thumbs. When she heard a sound she liked, he saved it as her ringer and locked the side button to keep her from turning the ringer off when she put it in her pocket. "You're taking your stuff?"

"Security blanket," she said with a shrug.

"But, you're coming back, right?"

She looked at his face and sighed. She dropped her bag at his feet and opened the flap. Inside, she dug out the one thing she had of Daniel's left. "This is Grape Jelly," she said as she handed him the small, purple stuffed elephant with a shaking hand. "He'll keep you safe," she whispered, repeating the words she'd said to the baby boy in his crib so many years before.

He took it carefully and looked in her eyes. He clapped his jaw tight and nodded once. He put it in his lap as she stood to leave. "Are you going to be ok?" he asked as she reached the door.

"Someday," she said quietly. "I just have to keep moving." She breathed deep as she pushed the pain back down where it belonged and left the room with a wave around the doorframe.

She rode the elevator down, bracing herself for the onslaught she knew was coming as it went. The farther down she got, the more the dread grew until it was creeping over her skin like a physical touch. Her heart was hammering in her chest by the time she stepped into the lobby and a cold sweat broke out as she turned the corner past the service elevator that went to the basement.

By the time she'd reached the back lawn and headed for a sunny spot to wait, she'd fought down the urge to flee. She still wasn't looking forward to Chantel's wrath. When Chantel arrived, she flopped down in the grass beside Jessie and stared at her. She wasn't sure where to start.

"How about the beginning," Chantel said sourly as she lit two cigarettes and gave Jessie one.

Jessie told her everything. Her life in Rankine. Daniel. Her arrest. Zack and Bernal. And why she'd lost her shit the night before. "When I lost him," she said as she pulled a ragged picture of Daniel when he was three out of her pocket and showed it to Chantel, "I couldn't handle it. So, I lied to myself for a year. Luke made me face the truth and I," she let the sentence hang. "I was running because I was afraid. But, he stepped in when I needed someone to stop me."

"Why didn't you tell me?" Chantel asked quietly as she stared at the picture in her hand.

"True facts?" she asked.

"Please," Chantel said as she handed Daniel's picture back and folded her hands in her lap.

"I've never had a real friend before," she admitted. "I guess I'm still new to the whole idea of trusting people not to look at me like I'm a monster or a science project. Or worse, like I'm broken."

Chantel punched her in the arm. Hard. Jessie winced and rubbed the spot where she knew she was going to bruise. She looked at Chantel in the eyes for the first time since she'd started talking and saw the tears staining her cheeks. Without a word, she let go of where she hugged her knees and reached out an open arm. Chantel leaned her head against hers and accepted the hug without hesitation.

Jessie exhaled. Now, she knew how Luke felt. It was weird. But, she liked it. "I'm sorry I hurt you," she said as they watched the sun start its decent behind the ridge. She hadn't realized how long they'd been out there.

"Don't do it again," Chantel said.

"I'll try," she said honestly.

"I can't believe you're living with the Lord of Darkness," Chantel said with a sigh.

"He's not as bad as everyone thinks," she said. "He's actually kind of... sweet. Ish. If it makes you feel any better I make his head hurt as much as possible."

"Leave it to you to find the biggest, nastiest badass on campus and make him your bitch," Chantel said with a giggle. "You pick that up in the hoosegow?"

"Honestly?" she asked as she laughed. "Being near the other prisoners used to rile them up too much so they shoved me in the hole pretty much the entire time I was in there," she admitted. "Too many prison riots."

"What's sad is I know you're telling me the truth, but I still can't picture it," she admitted. "You're too nice."

"Don't piss me off and you won't have to."

"Duly noted," she smiled and sat up. "Oh, I have to tell you. I met a boy last night."

"Why am I not surprised?" Jessie said with a smile and hugged her knees again as she listened to Chantel fill her in on her most recent adventures as a social butterfly until the sun had fully set.

When her phone started ringing, Jessie looked at her backpack and frowned. She pulled it out and looked at the screen. It was Luke. The son of a bitch had saved his number in her phone without her even realizing it. She breathed deep and answered.

"I need you to come home," he said by way of greeting.

"Why?" she asked. He sounded keyed up.

"I just need you to come home," he said sharply and paused. "Please?" he added in a nicer tone.

"I'm on my way," she said and hung up. "I have to go. Luke's got a bug up his ass and I have to go see why."

Chantel got up with her and walked her back to the lobby. "You think he'll let me come up?" she asked as they waited for the elevator. She thought about Luke's reaction to Chantel invading his personal space until the steel doors opened. He wouldn't be happy at all.

"Maybe," Jessie said with a shrug as they got in the elevator together and punched three and six. "But, let me prep him first. No offense, but you're not his favorite person right now."

"Is anyone?" she asked with a pout.

"Not really," she said. "I think he just tolerates me because he has to."

They said their goodbyes as Chantel stepped off on her floor and Jessie breathed deep as the elevator finished its ascent. When the elevator doors dinged and slid open, she saw the one face she hadn't wanted to see for a good long time.

"Evening, my dear," Bernal said with his ever present smile intact. "So glad you could join us."

"Bernal," she said curtly and glared as she stepped past him toward the apartment door and swiped her keycard. "To what do I owe the displeasure?"

"Oh, I just came to see how my newest Spirare is settling in," he said as if he didn't notice her attitude. "Mr. Interitus just finished regaling us with how splendidly you performed during your test yesterday."

"Has your ego expanded into the royal 'we' now?" she asked, not giving a shit that she was speaking to the one person who could evict her from the school. She shoved the heavy door open and stopped dead in her tracks.

Luke was sitting in his armchair with Grape Jelly clutched in his hand and a look on his face that told her he'd rather be anywhere else. And, behind him, looking out of the balcony window and the growing night sky, was a ghost.

"Daddy?"

J.P. Hart

Chapter 14

Her father turned around and stared at her as she hesitated in the doorway. Her eyelids fluttered as her vision started to swim. He gave her a pained smile and stuffed his hands into the pockets of his khaki cargo pants. He looked just like he did the day he'd been deployed for the last time. His strong jaw was clenched as his forest green eyes searched her face. His black hair was still buzzed to the skull on the sides and his wide shoulders were bunched as he braced himself.

She felt like her brain was going to fracture. With everything that she had been through in the last 24 hours, much less the last year, she wasn't sure she could handle much more. "You died," she said breathlessly as her heart and mind tried to reconcile what was in front of her.

"No, kiddo," he said sadly.

Not knowing which feeling to feel first, she dropped her backpack just inside the door and walked over to him. Luke stood from his chair as soon as she approached, but he didn't try to stop her as she hauled off and slugged her father square on the chin with all of her strength.

"You son of bitch," she yelled as he rocked back on his heels and almost went down. She was coiling up for another attack when Luke finally stepped in and popped her off her feet in a bear hug from behind. "Where were you?"

"Easy, focul iadului," he said in her ear and she struggled to get out of his hold. She kicked him in the knee and he grunted, but he didn't let go. "Calm down."

"I am calm," she said with a snarl.

"I believe you," Luke said sarcastically and started to push his calm certainty into her that she was going to kill her father if he put her down. She growled and tried to kick him again, but he shifted his leg before she connected. "Let him plead his case first. Then kill him."

"She does have spunk," Bernal said gleefully as he claimed one side of the couch and crossed his legs at the knee properly.

"Shut up," Luke snapped before she could. "You're not helping."

Jessie breathed hard through her nose as she glared at her father. He was rubbing his chin and staring at the floor.

"I deserved that," he said.

"No shit," she said. "Luke, put me down." He complied slowly but kept a light hold on her arms, flooding her with his strength and calm. "Explain. Now."

"Yes, Zadkiel," Bernal said from the couch, making Jessie stop breathing. "Please explain."

"Shut it, Bernal," Luke said harshly. "Or I'll shut it for you."

"Already so protective of your bond-mate?" he said with a chuckle. "Oh, how I do love being right."

Luke growled, but Jessie had tuned them out. She was staring at her father as the pieces clicked. "Zack?" she asked through clenched teeth. He looked nothing like her lawyer. He couldn't have been the same guy. "How is that even possible?"

"Think about it, my dear," Bernal said with a chuckle that scraped against her raw nerves like sand paper. "He's an angel. Imagine carrying the same face for eons. Not only is it dull, it's a quick ticket to recognition by the mundane world. The angels have evolved to be able to change their features at will if the situation calls for it."

"I couldn't let you stay there," her father said quietly. "I couldn't leave you behind."

"Again?" she whispered threateningly.

Her father winced and raised his hands in surrender. "Again," he amended. "I didn't want to leave the first time, but I didn't have a choice."

"Why?" she asked through her teeth as she gripped Luke's hand on her arm tightly. She was suddenly very grateful for him being there as she braced herself. Best case, he could keep her from killing someone. Worst case, she was pretty sure he knew how to hide a body.

"I didn't want to leave you, kiddo. But, angels have a job to do," her father said.

Her eyelids fluttered as a headache started to throb between her eyebrows. Luke had told her that her father had been an angel. It was the only way she could have been Spirare. But coming back from the dead to say he'd abandoned her because of his job?

"I've heard enough," she said, cutting him off. She shrugged out of Luke's grasp and started to walk away.

"Jessie, please wait," her father said.

"No," she said, but she stopped anyway and turned around. "You don't get to just waltz back into my life, just as I'm starting to put the pieces back together, and fuck it up with your sob stories. 'Angels have a job to do,'" she mocked. "Bullshit. You were too much of a coward to stay. You left us. You left me. In that shithole. Alone. Do you know what I went through? Do you know how many times I begged and pleaded God to let you come home?"

She marched back towards her father with her hands clenched at her sides to keep from punching him, again.

"I waited for you. For. Years. And you abandoned me," she said as she stared up into his eyes and watched him struggling to keep it together. "I needed you," she said in a low voice as another twist of the knife threatened to split her open. "Where were you when Daniel died?"

"I was on the other side," he said as he took a steadying breath.

"Yeah," she said with a mirthless laugh. "Right. Of course you were. Did you even care?"

"Of course I did," he said as his eyes begged her to understand. "I love Daniel just as much as I love you," he said. "He's my grandson."

"Then why didn't you help him?" she asked. "Why didn't you save my son?" It was the first time she'd called Daniel that out loud and the word ripped its way through her like a hot knife.

"I tried," he breathed. "But, I was too late. I tried to save you both."

"And what was so important that you couldn't get away?"

"What else could keep Daddy Dearest from his baby girl?" Bernal asked in a chipper tone. His voice grated on her last nerve and she twitched involuntarily. Luke was quick to grab her hand, lacing their fingers and squeezing tight as the rage inside her threatened to come to the surface, again. "Saving the world," he said, answering his own question.

"I couldn't even do that right," her father said. "I'm sorry, kiddo."

"Sorry is just an excuse not to get hit," she said. She knew it made her a hypocrite to throw his apology back in his face when he was seeking the same kind of forgiveness she'd just asked of Chantel. But at that moment she didn't care.

"Then how about this?" he asked. "I fucked up. But, I want to try and fix it."

"I don't know if you can," she said, shaking her head. She brushed past him and walked out onto the balcony. She needed to get her head on straight and being in a fish bowl with Bernal and Luke watching wasn't helping.

She folded herself into the chair she'd claimed earlier in the day and hugged her knees up to her chest in the seat. After a while, when she'd started to regain some semblance of calm, she heard the door slide open and closed again. A heartbeat later her father's hand landed on her shoulder.

She couldn't look at him as he came around and crouched in front of her with his hands on the arms of the chair. He stared at her with the same knowing, gentle concern that he'd had in his eyes when she'd told him as a child about the voices in her head.

"What?" she asked in defeat.

"I just wanted to make sure you were ok," he said.

"I'm nowhere near it," she told him honestly. She'd never been able to lie to him.

"Can I at least fill in the blanks?" he asked.

"Might as well," she said and rested her cheek on her knee. "I already feel like I've been emotionally sandblasted. I should at least know why."

"Your mother didn't know what I was, and I'd already told her I was in the Army as a way to cover my absences when I needed to tend to the Veil," he said quietly. "Every time I left, there was a chance I wouldn't be coming back, so I chose the Army as a way to make that easier for her to accept if the worst happened."

"But, it didn't," she said, getting angry again. "You just didn't come back."

"I wanted to," he said. "I got injured on the other side helping the others track down an artifact that had been lost a long time ago. By the time I was able to return everything had fallen apart and all I could do was pick up the pieces as best as I could. I never meant to leave you, kiddo. Please, know that," he said as he held his breath. "You are my heart."

He was begging. Something he would never do. She hated that she was softening, but he was telling her the truth. "So, where does that leave us?" she asked.

"That's up to you," he said and reached for her hand. He knew what happened when she touched someone and he was offering it up to her freely. Because he knew she had to know. She turned her palm up and let him grip her hand as she reached into his mind and heart. She closed her eyes as eons of memories flickered in her mind.

She absorbed the history of existence through his eyes and breathed deep as she reached her time. Love and joy filled her until she felt like her skin would burst as she watched herself grow from her father's perspective. Until the crushing sorrow of realizing he'd let her down crashed over her, tempered by the hope that he could make it right. Her cheeks were wet when she opened her eyes again and stared at her father. Silently, she shifted his hand and placed it on her cheek the way he had when she was a child.

His face crumpled in relief and he gathered her up in his arms. He buried his face in her hair and breathed deeply as she wrapped her arms around his neck and held him tightly, afraid if she let go he would dissolve into nothing. "I love you, Daddy," she whispered and she felt him shake around her as he exhaled.

"I love you, too, kiddo."

It was a long time before either of them could let go, but when Luke timidly stuck his head out of the sliding glass door to check on them she nodded and released her dad. He was there for more than just a reunion. She'd seen his other purpose in his mind.

"How sweet," Bernal said as they came back inside. He was still on the couch with his legs crossed, making her rethink her calm as she looked at his smug smile. "I'm so glad you could come to terms."

Luke had reclaimed his chair. She claimed the arm beside him and stared at Bernal coldly. "Too bad the same can't be said of us," she told him as her father sat down on the couch close by.

"Oh, do forgive me for my rouse," he said. "But, it was desperately important to me that you come here. And look what it's brought you, my dear," he said as he gestured from Luke to her father.

"Why is he here?" she asked her dad.

"Because he's my boss," Luke said.

"You're a teacher," she said.

"He's a Spirare first," her father said and Luke nodded in respect. "And one of the foremost in his field. Which is why I'm here, aside from my personal reasons."

Luke's hand subtly moved from the arm of the chair to her back, just under her shirt to her skin. Concern touched her heart as he tested her emotions and she let him in without a second thought. He exhaled quietly as relief chased his discovery that she was keeping it together more easily than she had before. She was still annoyed by the sight of Bernal's face but having Luke and her dad close by was helping significantly.

"You found the artifact?" Luke asked as she showed him what she'd seen in her father's mind.

Her dad's eyes widened slightly in surprise as he looked at Luke and then at her. She didn't react and neither did Luke. "Possibly," her father said. "There seems to be a pattern in the formation of the weak spots in your territory and we think it has something to do with the artifact."

"How big is your area?" she asked, leaning back into his hand to look at him.

"Mountain time zone," he said simply. "And a little of Central when needed."

"By yourself?" she asked with a look of disbelief.

He shrugged nonchalantly, but the thought of 'not anymore' floated through his touch as he rubbed her back slightly. She looked at him suspiciously and then back at her father as she sat up again. "Sorry," she said and gestured for him to continue.

"We think the Legions are trying to use the artifact to push through the Veil. We keep trying to track its energy signature, but it keeps bouncing from one side to the next, like their looking for something."

"Are you sure they have it?" Jessie asked.

"No," he said. "Not 100%. But, we believe it has been found by someone who knows what it is and what it can do. The fact that they keep jumping through the Veil tells us that they are looking for the one who can use it."

"I don't understand," she said.

"The artifact is a concentrated piece of the Primal Source," Bernal explained impatiently. "A stone that, if possessed by the right being, allows the bearer unimpeded access to all of the Primal Source's energy. In this world and the other, we are all limited in our power by the separation of ourselves from the Primal Source. The artifact eliminates that barrier and brands the user as a god."

"Shit," she said on an exhale.

"Exactly," her father agreed. "If they find the one who can use it, they can tear down the Veil from the inside out. And if they do," he let the sentence hang.

"Basically all the nastier bits from the Bible," she said.

"On steroids," he agreed.

"That explains the attacks," Luke said, and she looked over her shoulder at him in question. "Over the last year, more and more tears have been opening all over the world. The Spirare who watch over the territories are running themselves ragged trying to keep up and keep it contained."

"Then how do you have time to babysit me?" she asked.

"Kristoff has been covering my territory for the past couple of weeks. Gabby's brother," he said, answering her silent question. "Green," he shrugged. She nodded. "But, I have to get back in the field soon. The twins work better together and it's taking a lot out of them being separated for so long," he told her father.

"I know," her father said, "and so does their father. He's trying to help as much as he can, but the sooner we get you trained and cleared," he said, looking at Jessie, "the sooner he can get back."

"How long do we have?" she asked. She wasn't afraid. Unabashed pride swelled through Luke and into her at her willingness to take her new role in stride. The same pride reflected in her father's eyes, tinged with regret and concern.

"I'm not sure," he said. "It could be a month. It could be a day. Unless we can figure out where the tears are going to happen before they do, we're just going to have to crash-course it to get you ready as fast as possible."

Jessie took a deep breath and exhaled. Luke had told her Spirare were the angels' foot soldiers, but she hadn't known how little time she would have before she was drafted. "When do we start?"

"Tomorrow, focul iadului," Luke said. "Right now, you need to rest and a chance to balance out."

"I agree," her father said as he stood from the couch and looked at Bernal pointedly. "Get some sleep, sweetheart," he said as he leaned down and kissed her forehead. Luke didn't remove his hand from her back when her father came closer and his eyes cooled as he straightened and looked at Luke. "Lucifer," he said through clenched teeth.

"Zadkiel," he said back with an eyebrow raised in a silent challenge.

"You know," her father said as a sly smile quirked his lips. "Maybe, I should stay here. This was my home back in the day and it would be nice to be close to my daughter for a while. Help her train."

"I'm cool with it," Luke said carelessly. "But we only have one bed for right now, so I guess we'll have to share, inimioara," he said to Jessie as he slid his hand to her hip and smiled smugly.

Jessie groaned. "Fucking testosterone," she said shaking her head. "Put the dicks away, please. Dad, if you want to stay, you're welcome to. But, it's true. If you want to sleep in a bed, you're going to have to share with Luke," she said and smiled as both of them stared at her.

Bernal chuckled and her smile turned sour as she realized he was still there. "Actually, Zadkiel, if you'd like, I can let you in to the other penthouse. I believe it still has the master suite intact."

"Thanks, Bernie," her father said, but she was sure he'd rather Luke move into the other penthouse. He followed Bernal to the door but paused and snapped his fingers. "I almost forgot," he mumbled as he came back to her. "I brought you something."

"What?" she asked as he reached into a lower pocket on his khakis and produced a small velvet pouch. Its weight was surprising as he dropped it in her palm.

"Something that might help," he said and kissed her forehead again. "I'm proud of you, kiddo," he whispered and affection warmed her from the inside.

He smiled at her again before following Bernal out and closed the door behind him. As the door clicked into place Jessie exhaled, releasing as much of the stress inside her as she could, and slid to the side as Luke pulled her into his lap. She elbowed him in the stomach and glared up at him as he grunted and laughed.

"What the hell was all that about?" she asked.

"Angels are dicks," he said.

"So are you," she said. He shrugged. She rolled her eyes and lifted the pouch her father had given her, dangling it between her fingers by the silk ribbon tying it shut. "Do you think I can be ready?" she asked as she watched the pouch spin lazily.

"Yes," he said without hesitation and she looked at him. "Are you going to open your present?"

She pursed her lips and stared at it until he sighed and took it from her. He untied the ribbon and opened the pouch to peer inside. His jaw went slack as he looked at the contents and then back her. "Ok, maybe he's not as much of a dick as I thought," he said as he took her hand and turned the bag over her palm.

A heavy silver chain spilled out, carrying with it a pendant in the shape of the circle sectioned into the four parts. It was simple, but she thought it was beautiful and she smiled at it. "Instead of a class ring, I get a necklace?" she asked.

"It's the symbol of Spirit," he said as she examined it. "That particular pendant is one of only a few in existence, forged out of pure, balanced energy." He took it from her gently and fastened the clasp around her neck. The pendant settled in the hollow of her throat and her eyes rolled back slightly from the surge that rushed through her. "For a Spirare, it can help to protect you and enhance your power. Never take it off."

"Got it," she said breathlessly and looked back into his face. Dark circles hung under his eyes, showing her how much the day had taken out of him, too. "You need sleep," she said as she touched his cheek and felt his exhaustion. He put his hand over hers and pressed it into his skin as he closed his eyes.

"So do you. Come on, focul iadului," he said as he shifted her upright again and out of his lap. "Go to bed," he said and swatted her behind.

She looked up at him as he stood and started for the couch. Thinking about how much better both of them had been after spending the night so close to each other, she stepped into his path before he could lay down. "I thought you said it was a package deal."

"Are you sure?" he asked. He may have been acting like a possessive testosterone monkey in front of her father, but he wasn't going to encroach on her personal space without her permission.

"Yeah," she said with a shrug. "We're both adults and, as much as I hate to admit it, I slept better last night than I have since," she frowned. She hadn't had a nightmare the night before. As hard as she tried she couldn't remember the last time she'd slept through the night without medical aid, let alone without a bad dream. "Never," she said out loud.

He let out a mirthless laugh and shook his head. "Me, too," he said and lifted his hand in the direction of the hall. "Lead on McDuff."

She grabbed her backpack and shut the lights off as they went and she claimed the bathroom to change into her boy shorts and a loose t-shirt that hung to her thighs. He looked up at her as she came out and closed the door. He shifted back on the bed and flipped the covers back. She slid into the space he created and pressed her back against his bare chest. "Do you always sleep in just your boxers?"

"No," he chuckled as he reached over her and clicked off the light on the bedside table. "I usually don't wear anything to bed," he said next to her ear. "For you, I'll make an exception. And, I'll try to keep my hands to myself, but I take no responsibility for my actions if I'm asleep."

"Fair enough," she whispered back as her eyelids started to close without her permission. He slid his arm over her belly and laced his fingers through hers against her chest. The last thing she felt before the warmth returned and sleep claimed her was the press of his lips against her hair.

Chapter 15

Jessie woke up the next morning with a very large hand cupping her bare breast under her shirt. It took her a minute to realize it was Luke and had to resist the urge to smack him for being a pervert. He groaned when she started to shift his hand out of her shirt and rolled onto his back, releasing her from the cave of his body.

"Mai mult de cinci minute," he grumbled.

"Translation?" she asked, not expecting an answer.

"Five more minutes," he repeated in English and threw his arm over his eyes.

She shook her head and laughed.

It figured he would be a pain in the ass to wake up in the morning. She watched him for a moment, amazed at how the peaceful expression of sleep changed him. On impulse, she leaned over him and lightly kissed his stubbly chin. She had to dodge his arm as he reached unconsciously for her and she shoved the pillow she'd been using into her place.

He took the bait and allowed her to slide off of the mattress to her feet. She stretched and twisted to crack her back before shuffling out of the bedroom to the kitchen. She was going to need help to resurrect him. She needed his coffee bucket. She pulled up short as she reached the apartment proper to find her father leaning against the kitchen counter sipping his own cup and reading the morning paper.

She closed her eyes and opened them again, shaking her head to clear it. She still hadn't quite gotten used to the idea of his being around, and the normality of catching him in the middle of his morning routine was disturbing. "This," she said as her father looked up at her. "This is my life."

"What's your life?" he asked as she came into the kitchen and climbed up on the counter to get two mugs from the cabinet.

"An acid trip of angels in the kitchen and devils in the bedroom," she said as she hopped down and took the mugs to the coffee pot to fill them. Her father choked on the sip of coffee he was taking and she smirked. "How's that coffee smell, Dad?"

"Clears the sinuses, kid," he said as he wiped off his chin and watched her put sugar in one mug but not the other. "So, how long has this been going on?"

"I just moved in day before yesterday," she said.

"Yeah," he said as he crossed his arms over his chest and stared at her. "But, you two seem awfully homey together." She rolled her eyes and huffed. "Now, don't get offended, I'm just telling you what I see."

"He's my best friend, Dad," she said easily. It was true. She couldn't explain it, but she really was developing a serious weak spot for the giant pain in her ass. "He understands me better than anyone else and I feel better when he's around."

"But, he's Lucifer Interitus," her father said like the idea of being anywhere near him gave him the creeps.

"And?" she asked blandly.

"He's a cold, sardonic bastard with a mean streak that could give his name sake a run for his money," he pointed out.

"You forgot stubborn and hostile," she said as she sipped her coffee. He lifted his hand and gave her a look that said she just proved his point. "He also has a knack for being one of the kindest, most caring individuals I have ever come across. He levels me out and helps keep the worst of the crazy at bay. He's a good guy, Dad. Deep down. Like, center of the Earth deep." He chuckled at her and shook his head.

"You two really have bonded, haven't you?" he asked.

She thought about Bernal's constant digs about Luke and her being bond-mates and how defensive Luke seemed to get about it. "Why do I feel like I'm not getting the whole picture?"

Her father inhaled deeply and sighed in defeat. "Bonding is a connection that develops between Spirare and other Mancers on a Spirit level. Because you are in tune with the energy that binds all living beings, when you feel that connection develop, it's life altering. For your kind, there is no grey area. You're either family or you're not."

She thought about Luke and how quickly she'd made room in her heart for him and how devastated she would be if she lost him. The same could be said for Chantel, too. Daniel had left a hole in her heart, but Luke and Chantel were helping to mend it in ways she didn't think were possible. They were her family just as much as Daniel and her father were.

"Yeah," she said quietly as she felt Luke's energy start to swell and knew he was starting to wake up. A smile hovered at the edge of her lips as she looked up at her father. "I guess we are," she said and shook her head.

Luke shuffled out of the hallway in his boxers, yawning and scratching his chest. She chuckled at her father's sour expression when he saw him.

Luke looked nonplused for only a heartbeat when they locked eyes before his usual asshole swagger returned and he strode into the kitchen. He went straight for her as she held out his mug and kissed her cheek like it was the most natural thing to do.

"Why is there an angel in my kitchen this early in the morning, draga mea?" he asked.

"The balcony connects to the other penthouse and you two left the door unlocked," her father said with a note of disappointment in their lack of security.

"I'll be sure to remedy that next time," Luke said happily.

"Be nice," she said as she rolled her eyes and pushed herself up to sit on the counter.

"I'm always nice," he said with a sly smile.

She knew he was just doing it to be a dick, but she slapped his arm anyway. He laughed and leaned against the counter next to her to drink is coffee. Unconsciously, she rested her hand on his back and tested his emotions to see how he was. He'd been pulling a lot of bad out of her and she was worried that it was affecting him, too. He groaned and rolled his shoulders forward, silently urging her to scratch his back.

"Grizzly bear," she muttered as she complied. Her father watched the exchange silently and shook his head. "What?"

"Nothing," he lied. There was reluctant resignation in his eyes and Luke smiled smugly. "I'm going downstairs to the gym. You have half an hour before I come looking for you."

"Yes, Dad," she said.

"Sure thing, Pop," Luke said as her father set his mug in the sink and headed for the door. Zadkiel paused and hung his head in irritation but didn't say a word as he left.

"Why are you being so mean to him?" she asked as Luke set his nearly empty mug on the counter and stood in front of her with his hands beside her knees.

"I don't like angels," he said bluntly. "They're heavy handed ass-hats that fuck up their children and then throw up their hands and say 'what can I do?'"

"He's trying," she said and rested her hands on his shoulders.

"That's something, right?"

"Zadkiel is a rare case," he said and she felt the deep scar of his own abandonment brush her heart. She sighed as understanding came to her. He hadn't been so lucky. She didn't pity him, but she understood and slid her hands to his face.

"Take it easy on him," she said gently as he pressed himself between her knees and rested his forehead on hers. "Please? He's my Dad and I want you to at least be able to tolerate each other."

"Vei fi moartea de mine," he said with a groan. "You're going to be the death of me," he translated and nodded in defeat. She smiled at his martyred expression and kissed the end of his nose. Affection flowed through him and into her as he timidly leaned in and kissed her lips softly.

She froze at the contact and he pulled away to look at her. She hadn't expected it and wasn't sure how to handle it. Fear started to creep into his ruby eyes as she looked at him in confusion. She'd never felt that before. Sure, she'd loved needling him and making him uncomfortable with lurid comments and filthy humor, but she never thought he would actually feel that way about her.

"I'm sorry," he said quietly and started to pull away. "I overstepped. I shouldn't have assumed."

She didn't let him leave. He looked back her and braced himself for rejection. She didn't. Jessie cautiously slid her hands behind his neck and led him back to her. She closed her eyes and absorbed every sensation he gave her greedily as he fit his mouth to hers and wrapped her up in his arms. Their affection and relief crashed together and tangled through their connection and her heart thundered in time with his.

It felt natural to her to have him there and she smiled against his mouth. He tasted like coffee. When they broke apart, he laughed breathlessly and gave her a crooked smile. "Yeah?" he asked, still afraid she'd change her mind and put him back in the friend-zone.

"Yeah," she said and smiled back at him. "But," she said and pushed him away so she could hop off the counter, "if we don't get dressed and meet my dad downstairs, he's going to come back and I really don't want to have to explain us yet."

"He's worried about us being together?" Luke asked with a chuckle as he followed her back to the bedroom to get changed.

"Apparently," she said.

"Why?" he asked as he pulled his gym clothes down off their hangers while she retrieved hers from her backpack.

"Because you're a gigantic asshole," she said bluntly and he laughed. She turned her head to look at him and blanched at what she saw. Completely unashamed by the fact that she was sitting on her knees right next to him, he'd dropped his boxers and was bending over with his back to her in the process of swapping them out for clean boxer briefs. That's when it hit her that she'd never seen a naked man in person before.

A harsh blush crept into her cheeks as she stared the latticework wings that followed the hard v-curve of his waist and split apart to wrap around his hips to his knees. He pulled his boxer briefs up and followed the process with his jogging pants before he turned around. Her blush deepened when he caught her staring and gave her a knowing smirk, and she turned away to hide it. He chuckled and walked into the bathroom, leaving the door open while he prepared his straight razor.

While he was shaving, she shook her head and changed out of her pajamas and into her yoga pants with the cut hems and a sports bra. She grabbed her brush out of her backpack and held it in her teeth as she removed the ties from her braid and shook out the length. When she turned to join him in the bathroom, he was frozen in place with his straight razor just away from his chin and his eyes on her. "What?"

"You really don't realize how incredibly beautiful you are, do you?" he asked. She rolled her eyes and stepped up to the other sink to brush her teeth before tackling her braid again.

"You're full of shit," she said around her toothbrush as he resumed shaving. "But, I appreciate the compliment."

"I'm serious," he said and looked at her in open honestly. "I thought you were stunning the first time I saw you."

"Oh yeah," she said raising an eyebrow at him. "I make bat-shit crazy look good." She spit and rinsed her toothbrush before picking up her brush.

"Fair enough," he shrugged, "but, it's still true."

By the time he finished scraping his chin with the razor, leaving his face silky smooth, she'd managed to get her hair tied up and looked at him. He paused in the process of wiping the remnants of the white foam from his face and stared at her in question. She just shook her head. "You're biased."

"Maybe," he shrugged and leaned down to kiss her cheek. "But, again, it's still true."

She used her thumb to wipe the shaving cream he missed off of his ear and left the bathroom with him trailing behind her. She bent over to grab her sneakers and socks out of her backpack as she passed, only to jump back up and squeak as he goosed her ass. She threw her balled up socks at him as he laughed and left the room with his shirt and shoes in his hand.

Twenty minutes of snarky comments and grab-ass later they walked into the gym to find her father already warming up on a heavy punching bag. With the raw aggression he was putting into his blows, she couldn't help but wonder if he was picturing Luke's face on the bag. "Hey, Dad," she said as she came up beside him and watched his form. He was standing with his weight braced on his back leg and his resting hand away from his chest as he swung with the other, leading with his chest.

"Are you done fornicating?" he asked.

"Never," Luke said as he came up to hold the bag still. "What's the matter, Zadkiel? Don't like the idea of me doing your daughter?" Her father hit harder, making Luke grunt.

"Not particularly," he said between punches.

"Oh, lord," Jessie groaned. "I thought you were going to be nice," she told Luke.

"And, I told you I'm always nice," he smirked.

"You, nice?" Theo's voice asked as he came up from running on the treadmill. "Are you getting into the funny Kool-Aid again, brother?"

"Hey, hippy," Luke said with a half smirk.

"What's up, Satan?" Theo said with a jerky nod. "Morning, pretty lady," he said with a friendly smile at Jessie and leaned into her shoulder. "Who's the dude?"

"Theo, this is my father," she said as he paused in his assault on the bag to shake the Terramancer's hand. "Zadkiel."

Theo's eyes went wide as he stared at her father. "The Zadkiel? As in the angel that founded MERCE?"

"One in the same, son," her father smiled. "Pleasure."

"Holy shit," Theo breathed. "Yeah," he said as he shook himself and tried not to stare. He failed. "Pleasure, sir."

"See," her father said, turning to Luke. "Respect. He's doing it right."

Luke rolled his eyes and gave her father the finger. "Don't you have a tree to hug?" he asked Theo.

"Nope," Theo said as he started to recover from his awe. "Finished the whole forest before breakfast."

Jessie chuckled and shook her head. "Well, we have work to do," she said. "That is if these two are done with their pissing contest."

"We're done," Luke said with a smirk. "For now."

Theo didn't leave, though. As Zadkiel and Luke put Jessie through her paces, teaching her proper stance and form before moving on to sparring with Luke, a crowd had started to form. Jessie was a scrapper when she was younger and took to the hand to hand combat training like a fish to water.

"Stop holding back, focul iadului," Luke grunted as he flipped her off his back into the mat during their last match. "You're not going to break me."

She was drenched in sweat and sore as all hell by that point, but she grit her teeth and swung her body to the side, leading with her legs to sweep his feet out from under him. He went down hard with a grunt and she scrambled over to plant her ass on his stomach. "Ha!"

"You think you won?" he asked as he rolled and knocked her off of him. She went down on her hands and knees for a second before he wrapped one arm around her waist and popped her off the ground to hang upside-down at his side. She kicked and struggled in his hold, but she couldn't shake his grip. "Come on, draga mea," he said. "Get loose."

The blood was rushing to her head. "I'm trying," she said with a grunt.

"You have more tools in your arsenal than just your body," he said pointedly. "Use them." Irritation that she was refusing crept into her from his touch and she clenched her jaw shut. She didn't want to get in his head like that. She cared about him too much to hurt him that way. "Do it," he said harshly and flipped her over to grab her by the throat.

Panic flashed as her adrenaline dumped into her blood stream by the bucket load.

"Luke," Zadkiel yelled as he started to come forward to stop him, but it was too late. Jessie's instincts kicked in and she speared his consciousness with hers. She burrowed into his mind and pushed raw, searing pain through the arm that choked her. He slammed his jaw shut and bared his teeth as he took it. She pushed it higher up to his shoulder but his grip got tighter. He was fighting, pushing it back towards her.

Energy cracked around them as they struggled against one another. In the corner of her eye she saw her father holding Theo and a few other gawkers back as they watched. When the battle reached a fever pitch, Jessie felt herself open to the energy around them and pull in more.

Luke responded in kind, matching her surge with one of his own. The pendant around her neck burned against her chest as it started to focus the power into her intent. Zadkiel turned as white, feathered wings exploded from his back to shield the onlookers just as she pushed the energy out of her and into Luke with a shockwave that rocked the equipment in the gym off their platforms. His hold broke and he flew backwards onto the mat.

Jessie dropped to her knees panting as the energy leveled out and she was able to breathe again. Then, she looked at Luke. He wasn't moving.

She scrambled to her feet and ran to him. "Luke!" She slid onto her knees as she hovered over him, gripping his face in her hands. He groaned in pain as he opened his eyes slowly. "Luke, honey, look at me. Please, speak to me."

"Ow," he said as his eyes started to focus and he chuckled. "That fucking hurt."

"Are you ok?" she asked, concern pinching her face.

"That was fun," he said with a crooked smile as he touched her face. "Ready to do it again?"

She punched him. Repeatedly. When she was done throttling him, she smacked him in the forehead for good measure. He laughed the whole time.

"I think we should practice outside from now on," her father said as he came up to where she was still glowering down at Luke. He turned with a gesture at the gym. She looked around at the devastation and couldn't believe what she'd done. A crowd of students choked the entrance to the gym looking around with a mixture of shock and awe at the toppled gym equipment and then at them.

She shifted uncomfortably under their eyes and braced herself for the panic and fear she was sure would follow. At the head of the crowd, she saw Chantel standing next to Theo. Chantel smiled at her and started to clap. Theo joined her and soon so did the others. Jessie was confused.

"My best friend is a badass," Chantel announced as she came over to help Jessie up. "Remind me never to piss you off."

"That's his specialty," she said gesturing to Luke as her father helped him up, too.

"Yeah, but you love it," he said as he wrapped his arms around her shoulders from behind and kissed her cheek. Pride glowed in her chest from his touch and she smiled as she leaned into him. Chantel looked at her in confusion, but she shook her head. She knew Chantel wouldn't let it go, but looking at the mess they needed to clean up, she wasn't ready for the questions.

She stepped out of Luke's embrace with a sigh of resignation and went to help the others replace the equipment as best she could.

When everything had been set right again, the crowd dispersed with a few well-wishers congratulating them on a spectacular fight before they left. The whispers and excited chatter as they went made her wonder how quickly the rumor-mill would spread the details around the campus and she sighed. She hated being the center of attention.

Her stomach groaned and Luke's head swiveled at the sound. She hadn't eaten breakfast before coming down and it was already dinner time by then. He came over to her as she rubbed her belly and frowned. "You ok?"

"Yeah," she said. "Just hungry. Let's get out of here. You haven't eaten either and we all need a break."

He nodded and wrapped an arm around her shoulders as he led

them out of the gym to the main dining hall. Her father and Chantel joined them, chatting happily as they ate, and she was struck by the oddity of it all. She smiled quietly and listened as Luke exchanged barbed comments with both Chantel and her father, occasionally catching her eye to smile at her.

Her father grinned and told her how proud he was of her as he squeezed her hand before going back to chatting with Chantel kindly. She laughed and accused him of adopting her friend and Chantel preened. This was her family, she thought. This was her life as it should be.

When she felt someone watching her, she lifted her eyes to the entrance and spotted Dr. Jones with his expressionless face tracking her movements. When she caught his eye, he nodded once and left. She shivered involuntarily to dispel the creeping dread he left in his wake and Luke rubbed her arm. "You cold?"

She shook her head and leaned into him. Completely against his public persona, he kissed her forehead sweetly and hugged her tightly with one arm.

"Oh, how cute," Chantel said with a smirk as she looked between them. "Beauty and her Beast."

"Shut up, firebug," Luke said with a grumble and she felt his embarrassment at getting caught actually being nice.

"He snores like beast," Jessie said and smirked.

"I do not," Luke said, aghast.

Jessie grinned up at him and started to mimic loud, obnoxious snoring noises. He bit his lip to hide his smile and attacked, tickling her until she couldn't breathe.

"Jerk," she laughed and leaned into him again.

Chantel gagged.

"I concur," her father said, but there was a smile in his eyes as he looked at her. She lifted her eyebrows at him and he rolled his eyes.

When he shrugged reluctantly, she knew she had his approval. Whether he liked it or not.

Chapter 16

The next evening, after they were done training for the day, Jessie flopped down on her back on the couch with a groan. Two days of beating herself into the ground and she was ready for a vacation. Her father had promised her that it wouldn't always be so rough, but she was wondering if he didn't have an ulterior motive to making sure she was dead on her feet.

When Luke knelt over her and leaned down to kiss her, she had a pretty good idea as to why. She welcomed his weight and ran her hands up the back of his shirt, relishing the sensation of his pleasure as it crashed through her and mixed with her own. When they'd gotten home after their fight the night before, all she'd wanted to do was shower and go to bed. He'd begrudgingly agreed to keep his hands to himself as they slept, but she knew that wouldn't last for long.

She was nervous about going very far physically with him. She was still a virgin and was terrified that he'd be put off by her lack of experience. He didn't seem to mind, though, as he shifted her on top of him and took her place on the couch. Somewhere along the way he'd removed his shirt and her sports bra, and she blanketed his bare chest with hers as they started to settle down. "I'm sorry," she whispered as he held her and traced lazy lines over her back.

"It's alright, mândra mea," he said and she knew he meant it. "We go at your pace. When you're ready."

"I don't get it," she said.

"What?"

"Everything is moving so quickly. Not just with us," she said as she rested her chin on her hands over his heart to look at him, "but with everything since I got out of prison. I've only been here for a week and a half, but it feels like I've been here, with you, forever."

He breathed deeply and looked at her. His thoughts were jumbled, making it difficult to keep up with the speed at which he processed everything. Half of it was in Romanian anyway.

"Before I met you, everything seemed to blur together," he said finally. "My life was just a constant routine. Wake up. Work. Go to bed. Do it again. Because I only had to worry about myself, there really wasn't anything that made me sit up and take notice of how quickly the days were passing. Now, that I have you, everything is more vivid and worth paying attention to. So, maybe it's not that everything is moving quickly all of a sudden. Maybe you're just noticing how quickly it's moving for the first time."

"Yeah," she said as she thought about it from his point of view. She wondered if the bond was responsible for their feelings for each other.

"The bond helps," he said when she asked him. "But it doesn't dictate sexual or romantic attachment. That's all us. When Spirare bond, it creates a circuit of shared energy and helps us stay in tune with each other. We'll always need each other to survive because the bond helps us maintain our balance between light and dark. It helps us focus."

"Is that why I haven't had to deal with the crazy as much when we're together?" she asked.

"Pretty much," he shrugged. "A Spirare alone is volatile because they are trying to maintain their balance by themselves. A bonded Spirare doesn't have to bear the burden alone. When the bond happens naturally, our survival instincts kick in and latch onto it in whatever way ensures that it stays intact. If we hadn't been compatible romantically, we would still have been friends to the point of siblings."

"I honestly thought that's where we were headed until yesterday," she said and he chuckled.

"Only because you didn't want to see that us as lovers was an option," he said. "You have a rather skewed perception of yourself." She frowned. "It's true. I say you're beautiful, you say I'm biased. I flirt with you and you think I'm just being an ass because you don't realize how desirable you are."

"I'm not," she said. "I'm a bat-shit crazy, borderline midget with a napoleon complex, a filthy vocabulary, and a sarcastic sense of humor."

"That doesn't mean you're not desirable," he said bluntly. "It just means no one else has had the balls to pursue you."

"So, what you're saying is," she said with a smirk as she climbed up farther on his chest to look him in the eye, "you got me because it takes a certain kind of brave masochism to want to get in my pants enough to actually do something about it."

"What can I say," he asked as he sat up and leaned her back in his arms so he could cup her left breast in his hand, "you've got nice tits." He proved his point by taking said body part and teasing it with his mouth. She punched him in the arm. He bit her gently. She punched him a second time as her traitor hormones started to warm her again. He laughed and kissed her.

She was extremely close to just letting go and letting him have his way with her when his cell phone started to ring. With a growl, he took the offending piece of technology out of his pocket, looked at the screen, and threw it on the coffee table. He lifted her up in his arms as he stood from the couch and carried her back to the bedroom as she laughed.

"You aren't going to answer that?"

"Fuck them," he said and tossed her on the bed.

She was about to ask who it was when he caught the question in his mouth and scattered her thoughts. His hands were everywhere at once as he managed to get her out of her yoga pants and underwear in record time. He paused for only a heartbeat to stare down at her with a ragged breath before he reached for the waistband of his running shorts. The sound of a wrecking ball pounding on the front door made him stop.

With a very nasty sounding word in Romanian he glared at the door of the bedroom. She seriously pitied the person who was at the front door. "Do you want me to go see who it is?" she asked.

"No," he said with a snarl. "I'm going to fucking kill him," he muttered as he sat on the edge of the bed to swap out his running shorts for his jeans to hide his excitement. He didn't bother zipping them as he left the room with a harsh order for her to stay.

He was only gone for a minute before he came back, but the look on his face told her that sex wasn't his first thought anymore. "What is it?"

"There's a weak spot developing in the west woods," he said as he grabbed a shirt out of the closet and pulled it on over his head. "I have to go."

"I'll go with you," she said and slid off the mattress to get dressed.

"No," he said harshly and she frowned at him. He took a deep breath to calm himself and repeated more calmly, "no."

"Why not? This is what you're training me to do, right?" she asked as she finished dressing in a hurry before he could leave. He was on his knees at the foot of the bed pulling a long plastic case out from under it.

"You're not ready yet," he said as he opened the case to reveal a thick, curvy sword almost as long as her arm. He pulled the blade out with a sheath and attached them to his hip.

"I love you, Luke," she said, making him pause and stare at her. "But, I'm not letting you tell me when I am and am not ready. My pace, remember?"

"This is different," he said as he came over to where she stood fully dressed with her boots in her hand. He cupped her face in his hands and kissed her deeply. "I can't lose you."

"If you don't let me learn," she said seriously, catching his hand as he turned away, "you will."

His face locked down tight at her words. He was helping to train her to do exactly what it was that he was leaving her to do. And, theory only went so far. If she was in a situation where theory fell short and he wasn't there to protect her, she could be killed. He hated it, but he nodded and left the room.

She yanked on her boots and ran after him.

Zadkiel was standing in the living room by the couch when she came out, staring at Luke's shirt and her bra on the floor. When he saw her dressed and ready to go, his jaw clenched.

"Don't argue," she said, cutting him off before he could start. His jaw didn't relax but he didn't.

"Can you summon your wings?" he asked instead.

"I don't know," she said as Luke opened the door to the balcony. He motioned for her to join him and she did.

"Your instincts will draw them out," he said as he swung his leg up and stood up on the railing. He reached down for her and pulled her up beside him. "Let me go first, and then follow me." She tilted her head as he stepped off the railing.

Her heart caught in her throat as he dropped, but his wings exploded into existence after only a few feet. Behind her, her father stepped out onto the balcony and did the same. They both hovered in front of her as her heart thundered in her chest. She looked at Luke and took a breath.

She was weightless for only a second before the energy seared through her back and caught her with a jerk. She yelped at the sudden stop in her decent, and the pendant on her chest burned. Her translucent, black pearl wings beat slowly, reacting to her thoughts as she moved to join Luke and Zadkiel. Her father beamed proudly at her as Luke darted away towards the west woods.

She smiled once and followed with her father right behind her. Her wings were smaller than theirs, but she kept up with them easily as the crossed the back lawn about twenty miles away from the school.

"Stay back," Luke said to her as they hovered near an open meadow. "And stay in the air. I don't want you going in unarmed." She nodded as she looked at the center of the meadow. The air in there was wavering like a desert mirage and smoke was leaking out of it.

Flames licked out of the tear in the Veil and creeping dread spread over her skin. Luke drew his sword and the rippled blade began to glow as he charged it with energy. Zadkiel flew to the tear and lifted his arms to the sides above it. Storm clouds rolled in above them as he worked to close the tear, charging the air with electricity as lightning crackled through them. Whatever was fighting to get out roared and pushed harder as it tried to widen the tear.

Luke dove before she could blink as the first horn appeared, scraping at the hole in reality. The horn by itself was larger than she was, but Luke attacked with unbridled rage. The creature roared as another horn joined the first making the Veil groan under the pressure. Luke thrust with his sword as the creature's face came into view and it started to step out of the tear one hoof at a time.

It looked like a Minotaur infused with the boiling flames of Hell. Her father pulled his arms together painfully as the creature stepped free and allowed the gap to begin closing behind it. And, Luke didn't let up. He was faster than she could have believed as he landed blow after blow in the creature's burning flesh. But the thing batted him away like an annoying fly and reached for her father.

"Daddy!" she cried as it wrapped its flaming fingers around Zadkiel's ankle and yanked him out of the sky to toss him aside carelessly. Panic gripped her as she watched him tumble and the pendant around her neck flared to life.

Without questioning why, she lifted her left arm straight out in front of her as the energy from her pendant shot through her to form a shining white bow. She drew back the string with her right hand and summoned an arrow of pure light to aim straight at the creature's left eye.

She released the string and the arrow buried itself in the creature's eye socket with a sickening hiss. The creature bellowed in rage and clawed at the arrow as Luke swung with his sword to sever its horn. The horn tumbled end over end until it landed on the ground and dissolved in a churning puddle of flame. Luke swung again, but the creature caught his wrist and twisted it with a gut wrenching snap.

Without thought, her focus narrowed on the creature with a snap and she landed in front of it with icy calm. Her instincts pushed everything that made her who she was out of her skin and opened her up to the energy around her. She reached through the Void, through the Veil, through the ether that separated existence from the Primal Source, and called down everything it could give.

The sky above her churned and ripped with lightning as the energy struck down in a raw cascade of power. The creature tossed Luke carelessly to the side as the madness twitched inside her and she stared into its one good eye. Time stopped in the instant it took to get into its head. She burned through its mind with reckless abandon and seized it in her grip.

It choked and whined in her grasp. With a satisfied smirk, she lifted her hands out to her sides and swung them forward as her father had. As her palms connected, thunder clapped, and the energy she'd drawn to her rocketed forward, into the creature until there was nothing left to give. The energy expanded, stretching the creature's rocky flesh until it was shredded from the inside out in gory display of fireworks.

Her skin steamed with the residual energy left from her attack and she looked to the tear the creature had come from with her teeth bared. She reached towards it and snapped it shut with a twitch of her fingers. With the threat neutralized, she marched to where Luke had fallen, cradling his broken wrist to his chest and staring at her in open disbelief.

Her expression softened as she knelt beside him and carefully reached for him.

"Let me see," she said softly and nodded in encouragement.

Timidly, he moved his hand away from his wrist and she saw the burns masking the gnarled break site. She shifted closer to him and leaned forward to press her lips gently against the blistered skin. She let the remnants of her energy carefully caress his injury, healing it almost instantly where it touched.

He flexed his fingers carefully as she broke her contact with him and sat back on her heels with her hands on her knees. Her brows furrowed in concern as he stared at her with his ruby eyes still wide. He pushed himself up on his elbow and rested his forehead against hers, cradling the back of her head with his hand and stroking her cheek with his thumb.

She felt him push into her head, searching out where she was at mentally, and she welcomed him with all of the love and devotion she could find. "I can't lose you," she whispered through him. She meant it. She wouldn't survive if she lost him. He took care of her. So she would take care of him. End of discussion.

"I love you," he whispered as her father came limping towards them with his face a mask of confusion.

"What the fuck was that?" he asked.

"My girlfriend is a major badass," Luke said with a grin.

"And you thought you were scary," she said in response. "Are you ok, Dad?" she asked as Luke released his hold on the back of her head and let her go to him.

"I'm fine, kiddo," he said as he let her put his arm around her to take his weight off of his ankle. Luke came up on his other side and did the same, accomplishing more that she could because of his height and strength. "How did you do that?"

"Instinct," she offered feebly. "I didn't do it consciously," she admitted. "I just saw you two get hurt and reacted. I guess I didn't like seeing my boys injured."

"Can you fly?" Luke asked her father.

"Yeah," he said weakly and started to hover. He faltered once or twice on the flight back, but she and Luke were there to steady him.

When they reached the balcony again, Luke all but carried Zadkiel into his apartment through the sliding glass door and dumped him on his bed. Jessie climbed up on the mattress and removed his boots carefully. The swelling was starting to set in. She needed to stabilize it. She looked around the room as Luke clicked on the lamp beside the bed. When she found what she was looking for, she pointed at it.

"Grab his bag," she told Luke. He retrieved the battered olive drab rucksack her father had carried with him everywhere when she was a child and handed it to her without a word. She opened the flap and pulled the first aid kit she knew he would have out of its stretched belly. "Hope for the best and prepare for the worst," she said with a half-smile at her dad.

"Always," he said with a groan.

She popped it open and pulled a small splint with an ace bandage out. He had a full set of gear in there, including a field surgery kit that zipped up neatly in a leather case the size of his hand. She used the splint and bandage to stabilize and wrap his ankle and then reached back into the kit to see if he had any pain-killers. She found a bottle that rattled and held it up for him to see. "What are these?"

"Pure light energy," he said as she popped the lid and shook one out into her hand. They were white. And she'd seen them before.

"These are the pills they gave me in prison before the trial," she said and looked at him in question.

"Are you sure?" he asked as he looked at her in confusion.

"I know my meds, Dad," she said.

"That doesn't make sense," he told her as he took the pill out of her hand and popped it in his mouth. Luke went into the bathroom and came back with a glass of water to hand to her father. When he'd swallowed it and handed the glass back to Luke with his thanks, he settled back against his pillows and frowned. "Angels use them to heal injuries faster. But, taking them when there's no need would through you off balance. In an unbound Spirare it would be devastating."

"The first day I took it, I almost killed Dr. Faustus," she said quietly as she looked at her hands.

"Dr. Nguyen," he said out of habit and then paused as what she'd said sank in. "Who gave you the pill?"

"Olga," she said and she watched him stop himself from correcting her again. "She always gave me my meds."

"Was she a Slate?" Luke asked, making her frown at him. He was asking her father.

"Yeah, but not one of mine," he said.

"What's a Slate?" she asked.

"Slate is a slur against the mundane humans that are recruited to help angels and Spirare in their day to day," he father said. "They are usually those who are sensitive to the energy of the Primal Source but can't access it. The constant un-fulfillment of their potential usually drains them of hope, leaving them pretty much a blank slate emotionally. Hence the term. In exchange for their services, their employers will feed them energy that helps them balance out."

"So, why would she give me one of your pills if she knew what it would do to me?" she asked.

"Maybe she thought it would help?" he father suggested.

Luke looked like he was gearing up to pepper her father with more questions, but Zadkiel's eyelids were starting to droop. "Leave it for now, sweetheart," she told Luke and touched his hand. "Let him sleep."

He nodded and laced his fingers through hers as she climbed off the bed. Her father frowned at their grasped hands but didn't say anything. "Goodnight, Daddy," she said softly as she kissed his cheek and turned off the light.

"Goodnight, baby girl," he said and she smiled at him as she followed Luke out onto the balcony.

He led her by the hand through the sliding glass door of their room and clicked the lock into place before drawing the curtain securely into place. She sat on the edge of the bed to take off her shoes as Luke disappeared through the door and came back a minute later. He put his sword away in the case and slid it back under the bed as she stretched and looked at him over her shoulder. He caught her eye and a smile teased the corner of his mouth.

"What?" she asked as he came over to stand in front of her.

"I'm just amazed by you," he said down to her as he cupped her face. She pressed her cheek into his warm, rough palm and smiled at the feeling of his affection flowing into her. She really did love his sorry ass. He chuckled at her thought and leaned her back against the mattress as he blanketed her with his body and kissed her.

She was exhausted, but the feeling of his touch was waking her up in more ways than one. "What do you say we pick up where we left off," she whispered as he kissed her neck and slid his hand up her shirt to her chest.

"My thoughts exactly," he said with a growl and she smiled as he pulled his shirt off over his head.

It didn't take long for him to get her riled up and naked again, but she could still feel his restraint. He was still letting her pick the pace. She was shaking with nerves as he rolled onto his back with her above him, but he held her through the pain of her first time. His healing warmth wrapped around her and eased her until all she could feel was their pleasure crashing and tangling together, driving her to the brink until they shattered in each other's arms.

Panting and satisfied in a way she'd never imagined, she

collapsed against his chest and listened to his heart thundering in time with hers. They stayed that way, still connected and wrapped in each other's arms, through the rest of the night as they slept and woke to do it all again.

Chapter 17

"I don't want to get up today," Jessie said as she laid beside Luke with her head on his bicep and her back to his chest. The early morning light was beginning to tease the bottom of the curtain covering the sliding glass door.

"Me either," he said with a chuckle as his hand caressed her hip under the blanket. "We could call in sick." He faked a cough. "I'm sorry, Zadkiel," he said in his most pathetic voice. "We can't come out and play today. Why? Oh, no reason. Your daughter just fucked me half to death last night and we need a day to recover."

"Asshole," she said as she reached back and smacked him over the covers. He laughed and slid his hand to where he'd been all night as he kissed her neck and shoulder.

"Hey," he mumbled. "It's true. I think I got more of a work out with you last night than I ever have training."

She rolled over and threw her leg over his hip. He kissed her deeply and she grinned as she felt him start to nudge her again. "You're incorrigible," she said with a chuckle and then a gasped as he found home again.

"Yeah," he smiled wickedly as he rolled her onto her back and went with her. "But, you love me."

"I do," she said breathlessly as he started to move. "Now, shut up and kiss me."

He complied easily with a smirk and all coherent thought scattered. When they were through, she had to fight the urge to fall asleep in his arms again. Instead, she got out of bed to shower and get dressed. He followed her into the water and showed her he was just as talented standing as he was lying down, making her normally long shower routine even longer.

He also made it extremely difficult to get dressed until she'd half-heartedly threatened to sleep at her father's that night. He chuckled and surrendered but she knew it was only a temporary truce. When she finished making the morning coffee and brought his to his office, he pulled her into his lap and kissed her.

"Awe! Look at the newlyweds. SO cute," appeared in the center of the screen in green with a chime.

"Ah, man. Not fair," appeared in blue below it. "You get her and all I get it this pasty-ass shmuck."

Jessie chuckled when she saw it and Luke shook his head.

"How can they see us?" she asked as she looked around at the room for a camera. He tapped her shoulder and pointed at the monitor where a white light indicated that the integrated webcam was on. She waved.

Green: *waves back*

Blue: Woo Hoo! Attention from the female!

She shifted her weight in Luke's lap and grabbed the mouse to click the reply box under their text. "Hi, boys."

Green: Well, hello to the newest Spirare to join the ranks. Luci told us how well you did last night. Conratz!

Blue: Hey there, sexy lady. You sure you want to partner up with that ugly mug when you can have all this? I'll trade bond-mates.

"Sorry, honey. He's taken," she replied and Luke laughed. "Besides, I'm pretty sure his sword's bigger."

Green: Pwnd!

Blue: Ah, why you gotta be so mean? *pouts*

"Just good at it."

Green: Sharp, vicious, AND beautiful? DEFINITE keeper, Luci.

"Thanks, Kris," Luke replied, reaching around her to type. "I plan on it."

"I'll leave you boys to it," she said and got out of his lap. "Have you heard from Dad, yet?"

"Yeah, he called an hour ago while we were in the shower," he grinned and wagged his eyebrows as she rolled her eyes. "He left a message that said he *hoped* we were still asleep and to take the day off. He's going to stay off his ankle until tomorrow."

"I thought angels healed as fast as we do," she said with a frown.

"You and I heal faster because we have each other to draw strength from," he said. "They heal quick, but not that quick."

"I'm going to go check on him," she said.

"Ok," he said and she leaned down to kiss him. "I might not be here when you get back."

"Where you going?" she asked. "Just curious."

"I'm going to go back out to the meadow and check it out in the daylight. I don't know what it was, but I felt something else out there," he said.

"Anything major?" she asked as worry started to creep in.

"No," he said easily and pulled her back to stand between his knees. "So stop worrying. Go check on your dad and be naked when I get back."

"Horn-ball," she said with a laugh.

"I'm a guy with a hot girlfriend," he said as he slid his hand over her jeans and squeezed her ass. "Can you blame me?"

"Yes," she said with a smirk. "I'm your girlfriend. I can blame you for everything."

"Fair enough," he said with a shrug. "Now, go before I change my mind about letting you walk out of here."

She kissed his cheek and walked out of the room, pausing just outside the doorframe where the webcam couldn't see. "Hey, Luke." When he turned his head and leaned back in his chair to look at her in question, she flashed him and walked away.

"And you call me incorrigible," he called after her.

She laughed as she walked out to the kitchen to refill her mug and grab a second one for her father. Holding both handles in one hand, she went into the living room to the sliding glass door. But it refused to open. Frowning, she looked at the lock and saw that it had been clicked into place. That explained where Luke disappeared to before coming to bed. She shook her head and unlatched it to walk outside.

Her father was sitting outside of his room in a wrought iron chair that matched the set outside of her and Luke's apartment. His phone was on the table and his ankle propped up on the other seat. His hands were folded on his stomach and his head was leaned back with his eyes closed. He opened them as she approached and smiled faintly in thanks as she handed him the coffee she'd brought him.

"How you feeling, old man?" she asked as she leaned against the railing to face him.

"Old," he said with a chuckle and sipped his coffee. "How about you? You look different."

"How so?" she asked. She wasn't going to regale him with her sex-capades from the night before, but she was curious.

"I don't know," he said. "You just seem," he paused and looked at her closely, "happy."

"I am," she said easily and shook her head. "It's weird."

"How so?"

"I'd been sad and angry for so long, I forgot what this felt like. It's kinda scary actually. Like I'm waiting for the other shoe to drop," she admitted.

"Drawback of being a survivor, kid," he said. "You're always prepping for another disaster."

"I guess so," she said with a shrug. Unconsciously, the fingers of her free hand found her pendant and she twisted it lazily as she looked off into space.

"What's on your mind, kid?" he dad asked after she fell silent for a while.

"Daniel," she said quietly. She breathed deeply as her old friend loss popped in to remind her that no matter what she had at that moment, it could always go away.

"I know you miss him, kiddo," he said in a gruff voice and she looked back at him. Deep sadness was in his eyes as he watched her. "No mother should ever have to lose her child."

"He would have loved to meet you," she said as she wiped the moisture away from under her eye. "And Luke," she added with a chuckle. "As much grief as you two give each other, I think he would have loved Daniel, too."

"They'd be pretty evenly matched mentally," her father said, making her laugh.

"No, I think Daniel would be more mature."

"True, he would be six," he father agreed.

"Next month," she smiled sadly.

"Tell me about him," her father said.

He smiled as she talked about Daniel for hours, pausing to wipe her cheeks every now and then. When she ran out of things to say about the past, she told him about all the plans she'd had and the visions she'd had of him growing up to be the best man she would ever know. She talked and he just listened until she was talked out. She knew what he was doing. He was letting her get out all of the things she'd kept bottled up inside, helping her release her grief.

"Feel better?" he asked when she'd fallen silent again.

"A bit," she said, and she meant it. "Thanks, Dad."

"You're welcome, kiddo," he smiled as he put his leg down and stood up with a grunt to hug her. "I'm going to go lay down. I'm not as spry as I used to be."

"Ok, you need anything before I leave?" she asked as he walked back through the sliding glass door into his room.

"I'm good, kiddo," he smiled. "Just go enjoy the rest of your day off. We get back to work tomorrow."

"Sir, yes sir," she said as she took their empty mugs back to her apartment and put them in the sink next to Luke's.

She poked her head in the office, but he still wasn't back yet. She called Chantel to see what she was up to and got her voicemail, but didn't leave a message. She had the apartment to herself, but she wasn't interested in just sitting around for the rest of the day.

Making up her mind to do something constructive, she pulled on her boots and went to the lobby and out towards the back lawn. As soon as she was away from the students milling around outside, she closed her eyes and tried to summon her wings at will. It took a few tries until she got it right, but when she did she lifted off the ground and made her way over the west woods towards the meadow to find Luke.

She found the meadow easily enough, but there was no sign of him anywhere. When she touched down where the tear had been, she looked at the scorched earth with a scowl. "Bastard," she said to the ash that remained of the creature she'd killed. He deserved what he got for hurting her family.

When she heard rustling behind her, she turned, expecting to see Luke. But he wasn't there. No one was. On instinct, she reached out with her senses and caught the echo of life connected to the energy of the Primal Source coming closer. She beat her wings once and started to hover, preparing for an attack as the rustling got closer.

She narrowed her eyes as her pendant started to warm against her skin. She had no idea what she was bracing for. What came out of the woods was the last thing she'd expected.

Chapter 18

"Jessie," Luke called from the living room later that evening as she closed the bathroom door and rushed out into the bedroom to shut the closest door. She leaned against it and smiled at him as he walked in. "There you are, how's Zadkiel holding up?"

"He's fine," she said as he sat down on the bed to take off his boots. "How was the meadow? Did you find anything?"

"Nothing," he said shaking his head. "I could have sworn I found something but I lost the trail when it looped back to the meadow through the woods."

"That sucks," she said, gripping the doorknob to the closet tightly behind her back as she heard a low whine and scratching coming from bathroom. Luke frowned at her strained expression and she tried to school her features.

"What's wrong?" he asked as he came over to her.

"Nothing," she said and put her hands around his waist, subtly walking him away from the closet. He looked at her with one eyebrow low in suspicion as his hands found her back. "Kiss me," she said and he chuckled.

He complied with her order, but when the whining got louder his head shot up. She grabbed the back of his pants as he moved to pass her and he turned. She smiled sweetly and he frowned. "Luke. Sweetheart," she said as she pulled him back to her and slid her hands around to his back and put her chin between his pecs. "You love me, right?"

"Yes, draga mea," he said with one eyebrow raised in question.

"And, you would never hurt me, right?"

His face fell and his eyes narrowed. "What did you do?"

"Now, don't be mad," was all she got out before he opened the closet door and walked through to the bathroom. He'd barely cracked the bathroom door when a steaming black ball of fluff pushed past his shins with enough force to knock him of balance and darted around the bed.

"What the hell?" he asked with his brows pinched as he followed it. Before he could get a good look, it shot through the bedroom door and into the hall towards the living room.

"Puff," Jessie called as she ran after it with him hot on her heels. "Puff, come back here. Get off Luke's chair, you doof. You're still wet."

"Jessica," he said darkly behind her. "Why is there a hellhound in my chair?"

"Because he's being stubborn and won't listen to me," she said as she snapped her fingers at the squirming puppy. He wagged his feathery tail happily and danced on his big front paws. "Wait, hellhound?"

She looked at the smiling black puppy and his comically large, pointed ears and frowned. When he'd come out of the underbrush in the meadow her heart had instantly melted at how adorable he was. She'd landed and knelt down with a hand out as he'd approached her timidly.

She knew he wasn't a normal dog by his round, frightened red eyes and the feeling of the energy coming from him. But, he'd been so lost and afraid she couldn't help it. When he finally bounded over to her and licked her face, she'd immediately fell in love, scooped him up in her arms, and brought him home. She'd fed him the leftover steak in the fridge and given him a bath to wash all of the forest gunk out of his fur. She had been in the process of drying him when Luke came home.

"Yeah, hellhound," Luke said angrily as he brushed past her and grabbed Puff by the scruff of the neck. Puff yelped in pain and Jessie reacted instantly.

"Let him go," she said with a growl as her pendant started to warm against her skin. She may have loved Luke, but she was not going to sit by and watch him hurt Puff.

Luke's head snapped to her and his eyes widened as he set Puff back down on the chair. As soon as he released his hold, the puppy shot over to her and hid behind her legs, whining in fear. She glared at her boyfriend as she leaned down and gathered Puff in her arms.

"Hurt him again," she said with an open challenge in her voice. "I don't care if he's a hellhound or not. He's an innocent creature and I will not sit by and watch him be harmed. By. Anyone."

"He's a creature of the Legions," Luke said as he faced her and glared back. "He needs to be eliminated."

"Is that his fault?" she asked through clenched teeth.

"No," he admitted the same way.

"Did he choose to be a part of that world?"

"No."

"And has he done anything to warrant an attack or be treated like a threat?" she asked finally.

"No," Luke said, but his hard expression didn't soften. "But he could. He's dangerous, Jessica."

"So are you," she said and he winced. "And by your logic, so am I. Does that mean I should be *eliminated*, too?"

"No," he said with a growl as his protective instincts kicked in at the thought.

"Then if he goes, I go," she said. "Deal with it."

She didn't give him a chance to reply. She turned on her heel and marched back into the bedroom with Puff in her arms. She slammed the door and locked it before she sat down on the bed with Puff. Her eyes burned with angry tears as she hugged him to her chest.

"How could he be so cruel?" she asked Puff as he whined. "You didn't do anything wrong, did you?"

He sneezed at her. The doorknob shook as Luke tried to open it and she heard him groan in frustration.

"Open the door," he said. His voice was muffled by the door, but she could still hear his anger.

"No," she said and scooted back farther on the mattress until her back hit the head board.

She let Puff go and he walked down the bed a little before turning around to face her. He lifted his big paw up and dropped it with a yap as she watched him and then came back to lick her face.

When Luke knocked, much more calmly and asked her to open the door, she laid down and rolled away from the sound. Puff whined and jumped down to scratch at the door. She huffed before she went to pick him up and returned them to the bed. She curled up with him against her chest and buried her face in his soft ebony fur. She didn't care that he was still damp. He smelled like soap and campfire.

When the sliding glass door to the balcony opened, she kicked herself mentally for forgetting to lock it. Luke stepped in and she rolled away from him, taking Puff with her.

"Jessie," he said softly as the mattress dipped and his hand came to rest on her hip. She shrugged it off and scooted away a few inches. "Please, inimioara," he said in a pained whisper. "Talk to me?"

"No," she said, hating the tears in her voice.

"Mândra mea, I'm sorry," he said.

"Puff didn't do anything wrong," she said as he leaned over and kissed her arm. "He was all alone and afraid. He just needed someone to take care of him."

"I know," he said as he came closer and laid down behind her with his hand on her hip. "I overacted because all I could see when I looked at him was the things I've had to kill in the past. I've seen what hellhounds can become and I didn't want that anywhere near you."

"He doesn't have to be that way," she said quietly as she looked at Puff and saw the innocence in his ruby eyes. They reminded her of Luke's. "You aren't."

"I'm not a hellhound," he said.

"No, but you're ruthless and cold," she said and she felt him flinch. "You're a dangerous, cruel bastard. But, I gave you chance anyway and saw the kind, loving man you can be." Puff whined at her as she sniffed and inched closer to nuzzle her under her chin with his warm nose. "I just don't understand why you can't give him the same chance."

"I'm sorry, Jessie," he said quietly and rested his head against hers. He slid his hand up to the skin of her arm and kissed her hair as his remorse over his actions filled her. He opened himself to her and let her see the truth in what he said about his reaction mingling with the loving hope for her to forgive him.

She turned her head and he propped himself up on his elbow to look her in the eyes. She let him feel that she was still upset by his actions and he winced when he heard Daniel's voice calling out to her in fear. She'd heard it too when she'd found Puff in the meadow and realized he was just a child, abandoned and afraid. She couldn't let another innocent soul experience that if there was anything she could do to stop it.

He squeezed his eyes shut as the weight of his actions settled in his heart and realized the thought of him doing that to Daniel had flashed through her mind. He breathed deep to steady himself as he silently promised her he would never do that. To him, her love was sacred, be it for him, her son, or her dog. He would never do anything to harm it. Or lose it.

Puff whimpered in the silence between them and she released her hold. He hopped up and yapped at Luke.

"What, dog?" he asked gruffly.

"Puff," she corrected him as Puff put his paws on the side of her stomach and yapped at Luke again.

"What kind of a name is Puff?" he asked as he looked down at her an eyebrow raised.

"It's short for Puffy Little Bastard," she said begrudgingly as she scratched Puff's head. He danced happily on her stomach and rubbed against her hand.

"Of course it is," Luke said with a mirthless chuckle and she looked back at him. He was eyeing Puff warily. Slowly, he reached out his hand and Puff immediately went for it, forgiving him faster than she had. He sighed begrudgingly as he scratched the dog's head and neck. "Puff."

Jessie rolled onto her back and let Puff walk on her stomach to get closer to Luke. He stepped on her chest and put his paws on Luke's shoulder to yap in his face and lick him ruthlessly. She smiled slightly at his pinched expression. "See? He likes you."

"I noticed," he groaned as he pushed Puff off until he went to the foot of the bed and sat down. He wiped his face with his hand and looked down at Jessie. "Are we ok?"

"Yeah," she said with a sigh and rolled up to wrap her arm around his chest and bury her face in his shirt. "I'm sorry I didn't ask you before I brought him home."

"It would have been nice not to get blindsided by a new addition to our family," he said and hugged her tightly. "If you'd waited ten more minutes I probably would have found you in the meadow. He was the one I was tracking."

"Yeah," she said as she lifted her head. "But, if you had found him first, what would you have done?"

He just looked at her. They both knew if he'd found Puff he wouldn't have adopted him. "Maybe it's better that you got to him first," he said as he smoothed her hair. "At least text me before you go adopting anyone else."

"I make no promises," she said and buried her face in his chest again. She smiled as he chuckled.

"You have a big heart, my love," he said quietly.

"You're a big man," she said and he chuckled again. He shifted and she let go to look at him. As soon as she did, he claimed her lips and shifted them so he was beneath her.

"You know," he said with a sly smirk. "They say make-up sex is the best kind."

"Pervert," she said with a chuckle and kissed him again.

Puff yapped at them from the end of the bed and came up to squirm between them.

"This is going to get old quick," Luke said with a rueful laugh as he sat up and fluffed Puff's sides playfully. "Come on, Puffy Little Bastard," he said as he shifted Jessie off of him and picked Puff up to put him in the hall. "Mommy and Daddy need their privacy. Go chew on the couch for a while."

He closed the door and came back to Jessie with a devious glint in his eye. She laughed and welcomed him with open arms.

J.P. Hart

Chapter 19

The next morning, she woke up alone in bed and frowned. Luke slept like the dead and usually didn't get his ass up until after her. She stretched all the way down to her toes and got up to dress and search for him and her dog. She found them in his office. Luke was fully dressed with Puff at his side on the floor, chewing on a chunk of black rock.

"You're up early," she said in question.

"The dog woke me up," he said. He didn't sound mad. He sounded distracted.

"What does he have in his mouth?" she asked as she leaned against the doorframe with her shoulder.

"Charcoal," Luke said absently as he read what was on his screen. "Apparently, it helps settle his stomach."

"Did he get sick?" she asked as she came forward and knelt beside Puff. He thumped his tail happily in greeting as he gnawed on the charcoal.

"He ate a hole in the couch," Luke told her as he leaned back in his chair and reached down to pet Puff.

"And you're not pissed?" she asked in disbelief.

"I was at the time. Then I found out it was my own fault. I told him to do it," he shrugged when she tilted her head at him.

"Apparently, hellhounds understand human speech as well as they do their own language. At least according to Kristoff. He's the one that suggested the charcoal when Puff puked up a flaming wad of cotton batting on the balcony."

"Oh, shit," she said and stared at her dog.

"It's ok," Luke said. "I had a fire extinguisher."

"You're attitude has definitely turned around," she said.

"You know how he woke me up this morning?" he asked and she shook her head. "I heard a child's voice in my head saying 'Daddy, I don't feel good. I need to go outside.'" She froze. "Yeah, huge eye opener. You were right to protect him the way you did. According to this, hellhounds are Spirit based animals that are born from the souls that have been wrongfully trapped in the Veil. It wasn't Daniel's voice you heard in the meadow when you found him. It was his," he said gesturing to Puff.

"Holy shit," she said in disbelief and stared at him.

"My exact reaction, too," he said. "Along with a whole fuck-ton of apologizes to the little guy and a long, serious conversation about how big an idiot I am and how amazingly, incredibly wonderful a parent you are."

"And what was his reaction?" she asked as she scratched Puff's head.

"It's ok, Daddy. I love you anyway," she heard in her head in a child's voice. "Even if you are a big fat moron."

She bit her lip to hide her laugh.

"Thanks, kid," Luke said with a chuckle and patted his side affectionately.

"Why didn't you tell me you could do that?" she asked Puff.

"Not ready yet," Puff's voice echoed in her head. "Mommy needed time to tell Daddy."

"Smart little butthead, aren't you?" she asked and he yapped at her.

"Yup," he said and she laughed as she started to tickle his sides. She could hear a child's laughter in her head as he wiggled and yapped.

Luke watched them play with a smile and a strange look in his eyes. She raised an eyebrow in question. He shook his head. "Just thinking that Daniel was a lucky kid to have you for a mom," he said and she smiled sadly at him.

"Jessie? Luke?" her father's voice called from the living room. "Why is there a hole in your couch?"

"We're in here, Dad," she called. "Go say hi to your Grandpa," she told Puff with a smirk and he took off at a dead run with a squeal.

"Grandpa!"

Her father appeared with Puff in his arms and wide eyed look on his face. "Why do I feel like I missed something?"

"Congratulations, Pop," Luke said with a mischievous grin. "We had a kid. Aren't you proud?"

The stark terror on her father's face made her giggle, but she smacked Luke for it anyway. She explained to her father about how she found Puff and adopted him.

"Well, I could have told you that," he said when she got to the part about what Luke had learned about hellhounds.

"I figured it out on my own," Luke said with a grumble.

"So, who's going to babysit while we train?" Zadkiel asked as he hugged Puff and set him down on the floor.

"What's training, Mommy?" Puff asked as he came over and sat in her lap.

"Exercise, sweetie," she told him. "I can call Chantel."

"What's exercise?" Puff asked.

"It's like fighting, kid," Luke said. "Or Ann," he suggested. "Any of the Pyromancers would know what to do if he got sick again."

"Like you and Daddy did last night?" Puff asked with a whine. "Don't like it when you and Daddy fight."

"Not like that, sweetheart," she assured him and scratched his head gently.

"It's more like beating each other up, but enjoying it," Luke said.

"Like you and Daddy did last night?" Puff asked and then looked at Zadkiel. "Daddy says make-up sex is the best." She had to stifle a giggle as Luke let out a sharp bark of laughter and her father looked ill.

"No, honey," she said with a laugh and hugged his head. "Not like that."

"Oh," Puff said disheartened and looked at the floor before tipping his head up to look at Jessie. "Can I come train, too?"

"If we can find someone to sit with you, I don't see why not," Luke said as he rested his hands behind his head and shrugged. "Might learn a thing or two."

"Yay!" he said and started to dance in her lap.

"I'll go call Chantel," she told Luke as she stood and kissed him. Her father cleared his throat and she laughed against Luke's lips. He gave her father a smug smile as she turned away. "Sorry, Dad."

"Uh huh," he said as he followed her out into the living room with Puff leading the way.

She chuckled as she called Chantel to fill her in and ask her to babysit. With a delighted squeal, she agreed and they met her on the back lawn. Chantel played with Puff while they all stretched and got ready. Then, Luke turned to Zadkiel.

"Ready for a game of touch tag, Gramps?" he asked and summoned his wings. Her father grinned evilly and did the same. She smiled, summoned hers, and took to the air.

They followed her a heartbeat later. They spent four hours trying to knock each other out of the sky while Chantel and Puff cheered them on. Her father was ruthless in his pursuit against Luke, but by the end they'd seemed to finally come to terms and ganged up on her.

"Bravo," a cheery voice called to them with a faint sound of a single person clapping below and Jessie turned with a glare. Bernal was standing next to Chantel and Puff was hiding from him beside her.

Jessie was on the ground in a heartbeat and he ran to her to hide behind her legs.

"What do you want?" Luke asked as he landed beside her. Her father landed just in front of them, but didn't completely fold his wings.

"Oh, nothing," he said as he came closer. "I just came to watch the show. You're progressing quite nicely, my dear," he said to Jessie and Puff whined. "And you seem to be building quite the little family. I'm so glad I brought you here."

"We're busy, Bernal," her father said.

"I can see that," he said with his ever present smile intact and stepped closer. Puff whined louder and Jessie lifted him into her arms. He was shaking.

"I'm scared, Mommy," he whispered in her head and Luke's subtle step in front of her told her he heard him too.

"So, how about you fuck off and let us finish," he said.

"Don't worry, Lucifer," Bernal said. "I intend to. But, I did want to remind you that *pets* are not allowed at MERCE."

"I think this is a good time to make an exception," her father said as his wings flexed slightly in warning.

"Quite," Bernal said. He smiled and tilted his head. He locked eyes with Jessie and nodded. She saw his face twitch slightly when he looked at Puff before turning and walking away.

"God, he gives me the creeps," Chantel said as they joined her where she stood watching the exchange. "He's worse than Dr. Jones. What is his deal?"

"I don't know," Jessie said as she soothed Puff. "But, I don't like it."

"He's a bad man," Puff said with a whimper. "He sent the monsters after me."

"What monsters?" Luke asked at the same time she did.

"The ones like the one Mommy killed where I found her," he said. "It took me forever and ever and they were chasing me. I looked everywhere for you. But, then I found you. And you and Daddy and Grandpa and Auntie Chantel will keep me safe. He told me to find you because you were the best Mommy in the world and that you would keep me safe and I did and you are and you will."

"Who told you to find me, sweetheart?" she asked.

"Daniel," he said happily and her heart stopped. "He said you were his Mommy and that you would take care of me. He gave me his voice and his memories before he went into the light so I could find you and you would know it was me. He said if anyone could protect me it would be you."

"When did he tell you to find me?" she asked as her sight went wavy.

"When I was born," he said. "He gave me the big rock and told me to bring it to you so you could keep us safe."

"Luke," she said as the pieces clicked.

"Where's the rock now, Puff?" he asked as he flexed his wings protectively.

194

"I have it," he said. "It makes my belly hurt sometimes, but it's ok. Daddy gave me charcoal and I feel better."

"Chantel, grab the Masters and tell them keep an eye on Bernal and Jones. Quietly," Luke said instantly as he shot from the ground and hovered above them. "Then come to the apartment. We'll leave from there. Zadkiel take Jessie and Puff with you and get to Kristoff. We'll be right behind you."

"What are you going to do?" she asked him as worry speared her chest.

"I'm going to tell Kristoff to expect you," he said as he landed again to kiss her deeply. He held her and Puff tightly to him. "I love you," he whispered. "Be safe."

She watched him take off like an avenging angel and bit her lip in worry as a forgotten voice whispered through her mind.

My beautiful avenging angel. Will you burn with me?

J.P. Hart

Chapter 20

As soon as Luke flew away, her father herded them towards the woods. Her heart was racing as Puff asked her what was wrong. She wasn't sure. She knew she'd had her issues with Bernal, but the idea of him being after the artifact didn't make sense.

"I trusted him," her father said in a growl, more directed at himself than her. "After everything that happened, I thought he was fine."

"Dad," she said and stopped in her tracks, despite his hold on her arm. "Tell me what the fuck is going on." She didn't like being kept in the dark, especially when it concerned her family.

He father didn't look her in the eye. He ground his teeth, making the muscle in his jaw jump. His mind was a rat's nest of betrayal and disbelief. And shame.

He opened his mouth to speak, only to close it and huff. He shook his head and tried to move her again, but she dug her heels in and refused to budge. "Talk to me, Zadkiel," she said. It wasn't a request. He winced at her use of his real name and exhaled in defeat.

"When we go to the Other Side, the angels are supposed to have at least one Spirare with them," he said. "Bernal was my partner on my last assignment." Pain and regret swirled in his mind and he had to breathe deeply to steady himself. "We were attacked by the Legions. He almost died defending me. We can fight if we need to, but angels aren't Spirare. We don't have the instincts that you do.

That leaves us vulnerable," he winced and shifted his shoulders. "They tore my wings out and left me to die."

Jessie felt ill. Her wings came and went as pure energy, but she could still feel them as if they were solid. His *were* solid. She'd seen the way they attached to his back by flesh and bone when he called them out.

"They captured Bernal," he continued. "They held him hostage and tortured him, feeding him dark energy to throw off his balance. They believed that the angels had the artifact and that they could use him to trade for it."

"But, you didn't have it," she said. "You lost it."

"They didn't know that. We've been searching for it for almost two thousand years if you go by time on this side. In the Void," he shook his head when she looked at him in confusion. "On this side, I was only gone for nine years from the time that I said goodbye to you to the time I got back. In the Void, I was gone for over four hundred thousand millennia."

"Shit," she said breathlessly. The idea that he would spend that long away from her and still care as much as he did was incredible. A lesser man would have forgotten her and moved on. "Dad," she said as her heart ached for him.

He shook his head. He didn't want her to feel sorry for the time he lost in the Void. But he did need her to understand. "The others found me not long after we'd been attacked and took me through to the Other Side and to the healers that knew us. They helped me regrow my wings, but the whole time I was gone, they had him."

Jessie tried to wrap her head around it and failed. She couldn't see how anyone could have survived that. When she was off balance, the voices in her head threaten to tear her apart from the inside out. The idea of being force fed darkness to prevent her from regulating was unthinkable. "How did you get him back?"

"The angel Michael went to the Legions' stronghold in the Void and claimed that he would give them the artifact if they spared him.

When they gave him Bernal, he gave them a stone he'd imbued with a part of his soul. It weakened him, but they fell for it and he was able to get away.

"When we got him back, he was broken. His balance was so far gone all we could do was try to help him regulate it. Michael developed the light pills with the healers that had helped me. He gave them to Bernal to try and level him out. It seemed to work. He seemed like his old self.

"Bernal was," her father shook his head and stared back in the direction of the school. "He used to be the best Spirare, the best man, I had ever known. I trusted him like a brother. I didn't like the way he manipulated you into coming here, but I trusted him when he told me he would help you.

"He's always made it his mission to help as many novice Spirare as he could," he said and shrugged. "I always thought it was because he was looking for a bond-mate to help him. He was regaining himself, but the imbalance never seemed to let him rest. I think the darkness that infected him while he was held captive warped his soul. If that's true, then the Legions could have won him over to their cause."

"But, why would he do this to us now?" she asked as she shifted Puff's weight in her arms. "To Puff?"

"When Luke was researching the increase in weak spots, he noticed that most of the ones that resulted in an attack of some kind, the ones that were created by the Legions trying to push through, happened simultaneously."

"Like they were trying to keep you busy," she said.

"Or they were trying to hide the real pattern," he said with a nod. "The sheer volume of the attacks is what lead us to believe they were testing our responses, but now I'm wondering if it was because they were trying to hide the fact that they were looking for Puff."

Jessie remembered the maps on Luke's computer and the virtual pins he'd placed. "There was a higher concentration of attacks near

Rankine before the trial. And then it started travelling north."

Her father nodded. "Now that I know Puff was looking for you, it makes sense."

"He's not getting Puff," she said. End of story.

"I don't doubt your ability to fight," he said. "But, as much as it pains me to say it, I agree with Luke. We need to get you somewhere safe. Kristoff is the closest Spirare in the area aside from you and Luke. And the more of you there are, the better."

"Then lead the way," she said.

"We'll travel using the edge of the Veil. We won't go far enough to get pulled into the Void, but it will be faster than flying," he said and pulled her deeper into the trees until they were out of sight.

He lifted his hand and the air started to waver. It was like the tear the night she'd killed the creature, but it felt more superficial. He curled his right wing around her and Puff with a deep breath. "This will be like your test but only for a heartbeat," he said. "Brace yourself."

"Will Puff be alright?" she asked as fear shot through her, making her muscles clench.

"I'll be alright, Mommy," he said. "The rock took me through there before. It's pretty like your wings."

She exhaled slowly and nodded to her father. She stepped with him into the Veil and held her breath.

No sooner had they stepped into the Veil than they stepped out and into a blistering cold wind. Kristoff was in a cabin deep in the peaks of the northern Rocky Mountains and an early season storm was moving in. She curled her wings protectively around herself and Puff as her father tried to shield them both with his own and led them towards the building a few yards away.

The door to the structure opened as soon as they came into sight and a man filled the frame waiting for them. As she stepped closer and recalled her wings, she could see his round, grizzled face. He wasn't as tall as Luke, but that wasn't by much. He was also much softer around the middle. His shaggy brown hair hung to his jaw and his bright blue eyes were grinning. He opened his arms and gathered her in a bear hug as soon as she stepped onto the porch.

"Mrs. Lucifer!" he said as he popped her off her feet like she weighed nothing and wasn't carrying thirty pounds of hellhound in her arms. "So glad to finally meet you! Come in. Come in. I just got off the phone with Luci," he said as he ushered them in and closed the door. "He's got your friend and he's on his way. They should touch down in a few hours if the weather stays good."

"They're flying through this?" she asked.

"Pyromancers can't travel by Veil, sweetheart," her father said. "The other Mancers can't handle the shift in energy."

"Zack, my man," Kristoff said as if he'd just noticed her father's presence and gathered him into a bear hug hard enough to crack his back. "How you been, brother?" he asked as he set her father back on his feet.

"Good, Kris, good," he said with a good natured groan. "How are you holding up?"

"Meh," he said with a shrug. "I'll feel better when the Gabes get here."

"Gabes?" she asked.

"His brother and their father," Zadkiel answered her. "They're both named Gabriel."

"Hey, did you tell Luci that Mike's on his way, too?" Kristoff asked with a pained expression.

"I didn't know he was," he said with a frown.

"Oh, shit, maybe I was the one that was supposed to tell him," he said. He frowned hard and winced. His hand twitched and he started smacking his forehead repeatedly to a chorus of, "Shut up.

Shut up. Shut. Up."

"Is it that bad after only a few weeks?" her father asked.

Kristoff shrugged with a wan smile. "It comes and goes."

"Oh, honey," Jessie said as understanding dawned.

Without his bond-mate to balance him, the voices were getting bad. She leaned against his arm with her cheek and tried to ease him through her touch. They may not have been bond-mates, but his features did seem to relax a bit.

"Thanks, doll," he said with a sigh of relief and hugged her with one arm. "I needed that. If Luci doesn't wife you, I might have to."

"What does that mean, Mommy?" Puff asked with a yawn.

"You had puppies?" Kristoff asked with a grin. "Mosel tov. I always knew Luci was a dirty dog. And what's your name, little guy?"

"Puffy Little Bastard," he said innocently and Kristoff laughed. "But, Mommy and Daddy call me Puff."

"Well, it's a pleasure to meet you," he said and put out his hand. "I'm your Uncle Kris." Puff put his paw in Kris's palm and he shook it. "Now, come in and sit by the fire. Are you hungry? Thirsty? I just made some hot cocoa."

Jessie shook her head as she let him lead her to a blanket in front of a roaring fire place. Kristoff fused over them like a mother hen for almost an hour while her father was on and off the phone pacing in front of the windows. Puff was fast asleep in her arms when the door opened again and her head shot up, hoping it was Luke and Chantel.

Another large man stepped in instead and stomped the snow off his boots on the rug. He was the carbon copy of Kristoff, save for the fact that he kept his hair shorter and his beard trimmed neatly. "Honey, I'm home."

"Brother," Kristoff said in happy relief as he got up from the couch and gathered his twin in a strong hug. They both seemed to relax significantly as they put their foreheads together for a minute before breaking apart.

"You look like shit, brother-man," Gabby said with a smile.

"I always look like shit," Kris said. "I look like you."

Gabby chuckled and clapped a hand on his brother's shoulder. A tall, slim man with platinum blonde, curly hair and a cherub face stepped through the door and shut it behind him. He smiled at the twins and accepted another bear hug from Kristoff with a good natured laugh. "Calm down, Kris, you just saw me two days ago."

"I know, Dad," he said. "I'm just glad you guys got here safe. I was getting worried."

"We're fine, son," Gabriel assured him. Jessie smiled at the exchange and shifted Puff in her arms as he yawned and nuzzled into her. "And, who is this?" Gabriel asked as he smiled at her and he came around the couch.

As he came closer and saw what she was holding, his step faltered a little. She saw the same concern that had colored Luke's features at first, but he smothered it and searched her face. "He's ok," she whispered. "Promise."

"Mommy?" Puff asked with a tired yawn as she shifted to shake Gabriel's hand and introduce herself. "Where's Daddy?"

"He'll be here soon, sweetheart," she said softly and kissed his muzzle. "Go back to sleep."

"Ok," he said and was asleep before he finished the thought.

"He's had a lot of excitement today," she explained to Gabriel as he crouched down beside them. His sparkling blue eyes smiled as he looked at her. "Poor guy."

"He's in good hands, though," he said. "How are you holding up?"

"I'll be better when Luke is here," she said. They'd only been separated for a short time, but the distance was killing her. The voices had begun to nag at the edges of her mind as soon as she'd stepped out of the Veil. She didn't know how the twins had handled it.

"Why don't you go get some rest?" her father asked as he came over from the window to greet Gabriel. "I can take the baby for now."

She shook her head at his offer, but let him and Gabriel help her to her feet. Gabriel led her to a small room in the back of the cabin with a full sized mattress covered in a thick quilt. Her father and Gabriel did a sweep of the room, making sure to check every nook and cranny.

"Is it really that dangerous?" she asked quietly.

"The Veil exists everywhere," Gabriel said. "This cabin is warded against disruptions, but we don't want to take any chances if we can help it."

"If the rock Puff has is the artifact, and Bernal is after him for it," her father said and let the sentence hang. "I just hope Luke and Chantel managed to get out of there without tipping him off."

Jessie closed her eyes and wished for the millionth time that Luke would arrive soon. Not just for his safety or hers, but for Puff's. If Daniel had sent him to her, then nothing was going to stand in her way to keep him safe. On reflex, she summoned her wings as soon as she settled with him against her chest and covered him from view. He was snoring softly, and she got lost in the gentle rhythm as the angels left the room and closed the door. She hadn't intended to sleep. She'd only closed her eyes to rest for a while and try to get the noise in her head to calm down, but soon she drifted off, too.

Chapter 21

Jessie woke up to the feeling of her wing being shifted gently and the mattress dipping beside her. Warmth flooded her as Luke's rough touch, still cool from being outside, drifted over her hip to her back and his lips brushed her cheek. She felt his wing wrap over hers as he settled down with Puff between them. "Hi," he whispered when her eyes opened.

Her relief and affection chased his love through her veins at the sound of his voice. "Hey," she whispered back.

"How you feeling?" he asked, even though he didn't have to.

"Better," she said as he rested his forehead against hers and she brushed her nose against his. "You?"

"Better," he said and kissed her softly. "How's the pup?"

"Brave," she said with a rueful chuckle. "He really loves you a lot, by the way."

"Yeah," he chuckled. "The Puffy Little Bastard is really growing on me, too," he said softly as he gently rubbed Puff's ear. "I never thought about being a father or having a real family before," he whispered, more to himself than to her. "I didn't think it would ever be an option for me," he looked back at her with an oddly pained expression. "But, now that you two are here, I couldn't picture my world without you in it."

"Don't worry," she said softly and smiled. "I won't tell anybody you're turning into a big softy."

"Thanks for that," he said with a chuckle and kissed her again. "Wouldn't want anyone knowing I have a heart."

They laid like that for what seemed like an eternity, until a soft knock at the door turned it into a heartbeat. Luke rolled off the mattress and answered the door as Puff started to wake up with a stretch. He spoke with someone in a low voice for a moment or two before closing the door and turning back just in time for Puff to realize he was there. "Daddy!" he said with an excited squeal and hopped off the bed to jump on Luke's legs.

"Hey, little guy," he said with a smile and bent at the waist to pick him up as he recalled his wings. Puff licked his face ruthlessly as he laughed. "I missed you. Did you do a good job protecting Mommy while I was gone?"

"Yup," he said proudly as he wagged his fluffy tail. "And Uncle Kris and Grandpa, too!"

"He did such a good job," she said indulgently as she smiled at them. "In fact, he did so well he completely missed the Gabes."

"Who?" Puff asked and she chuckled.

"More than that," Luke corrected with a look that told her he wasn't happy. "Michael just got here."

"Another Spirare?" she asked with a frown.

"Worse," he said darkly. "Another angel."

She stared at him for a minute before she recalled her wings and joined him at his side. He opened the door and let her lead as he carried Puff in his arms. When Jessie saw the newest arrival, understanding smacked her in the head hard enough to make her eyes cage. He was six and a half feet tall and built like a brick shit-house. His long black hair was pulled loosely from his hard, square jaw and his violet eyes were as cold as ice as he turned to look at her.

When his eyes drifted to Luke, they flared for only a moment before returning to cool calculation. "Son," he said with a curt nod.

"Michael," Luke said back through clenched teeth. His hand found Jessie's shoulder protectively and she fed him as much strength as she could.

"Who's that, Daddy?" Puff whispered and Michael's eyes narrowed at him. She didn't like the way he was looking at him and her pendant started to warm in response.

"No one important, sweetheart," she answered Puff loud enough for Michael to hear and his eyes snapped to hers. She raised an eyebrow in silent challenge and stared back.

He looked away first, under the guise of addressing the others. "Shall we get this over with?"

"Get what over with?" she asked as she and Luke took Puff into the main seating area. Luke handed him back to her as she settled near the fire where Chantel was holding her hands in the flames and shivering. She paused for a moment to hug Jessie and Puff before she went back to thawing out.

"Bloody Big Bird," she muttered. "Wouldn't slow down until I thought my face would freeze off."

"I am under the understanding that your," he paused and looked at Puff whose ears drooped with a whine, "*pet* is currently in possession of the artifact. If that's true, then I believe it's time we have it back so that it can be protected properly."

"By the same ones who lost it in the first place," Luke said from where he stood with his arms crossed over his chest beside her. "You don't see the flaw in that logic?"

"We are much better equipped to protect the piece of the Primal Source than any Mancer," he said to his son, but Jessie saw the ire flash in his eyes. "We are stronger than your kind, and therefore can handle its power better."

"Bigger guns don't mean better defense," her father said.

207

"Understanding the power and the drive to protect it does."

"And you think the Spirare have what it takes to keep it safe from the Legions," Michael said sarcastically.

"I do," Gabriel said with a nod to Jessie. "If the pup has it, they'd destroy anything in their path to keep them both safe. Any good parent would."

"That *thing* is not their son," Michael said harshly and she bristled.

"Like you really have room to talk about parenting?" she said callously. His jaw snapped shut with an audible clack as he glared at her with open threat. As she stared at him she felt a faint pulse brush against her skin and her pendant started to warm again. Something about him was off. It was barely there, but she could feel it. "You want it for yourself. Don't you?"

"How dare you," he said on a hiss.

"That's it, isn't it?" she asked as she handed Puff to Chantel and got to her feet. She could feel it, stirring under the surface. It teased the malicious voice back into her mind as it whispered in excitement. Her hand twitched at her side as she stepped closer to Michael and a smirk stretched her lips. "You want it so you can use it for yourself."

"And, why would I want that?" he asked as he faced her with narrowed eyes.

"You've been tainted by the darkness," she said as the malicious voice pressed the thought into her mind. "You're desperate. You're losing your soul. It couldn't handle being fractured in the Void and you want the artifact to get it back."

"How," he started to ask, but she cut him off.

"And, how exactly do you plan on getting it?" she asked as the malicious voice prompted her. *Ittybittybitsittybittybits*

"I'll cut it out if I have to," he said as she slipped briefly into his mind and drew the truth from his lips.

Luke bristled, but he didn't need to worry. That was all Jessie needed to hear. She shoved her way into Michael's brain like a charging bull and seized ahold of him.

His violet eyes peeled wide in shock at the violation an instant before the vision took hold. She pressed an image of darkness wrapping around his neck, feeling its way into his eyes and down his throat, into his mind. He started to choke, clawing at his skin in desperation. The satisfaction of knowing his greatest fear and exploiting it made her smile.

"Threaten my family again," she whispered as he stared in unblinking terror. "I know what haunts you. I will make you live it for eternity. Don't. *Fuck*. With. Me."

For good measure, she let the others see what she was showing Michael. Just in case there were any doubts as to how serious she was.

"Jessie," Luke said as he gripped her shoulder and pressed his calm reassurance that she'd made her point into her.

She relaxed and dropped him instantly. When he fell to his knees hacking, a small orange bottle rattled to the floor from his coat pocket. Her father was the one to pick it up and shook the pills into his palm. They were the same white pills he carried in case of injury.

"Michael?" he asked in disbelief.

"He's been using them to keep the darkness at bay," she said as Michael continued to wheeze. "Looks like Mikey has been keeping too many secrets."

"Dude," Gabby said, breaking the tense silence in the cabin. "Is it just me, or was that hot as hell?"

"I can't take you anywhere," Kris said ruefully.

Michael refused to meet her eyes again after that, which was fine with her. She didn't need his acceptance or approval. She'd seen in his mind that he'd become infected by the darkness in his pursuit to get closer to the Primal Source. He was the strongest of the angels, but that hadn't been enough. He'd wanted more. He'd wanted to be the strongest being in existence because he thought it was the best way to protect it.

"If it wasn't for the fact that you pulled that directly from his brain," Luke said later after she'd told him what she'd seen, "I wouldn't believe you."

He was sitting on the bed, covering Puff's eyes, as he watched her change into the clean clothes he'd brought for her. She hadn't had the chance to purchase anything warmer than a sweater back at MERCE, so he'd brought her one of his hooded sweatshirts. It fit her like a dress but it was comfy as fuck and it smelled like him. It was navy blue with an image of a college logo for S.T.F.U. University. Had it not been for the Spartan with a ball gag in its mouth, she would have thought it was a real college.

"Would you believe me that his image of existence is you?" she asked as she climbed up onto the bed beside him.

"He has a funny way of showing it," he said sourly.

She kissed the pout off his face. "I'm not expecting you to make up at any point," she said. "He's still a gigantic prick no matter how good his intentions were. But, just know that the mistakes he's made were for the right reasons."

Luke groaned and hung his head. She put her forehead against his temple and her arms around his shoulders.

"Why are angels so stupid, Mommy?" Puff said with a tiny sneeze. Luke chuckled.

"He's your son," she told Luke.

"Good boy," he said as he scratched Puff's head and winked at her. She smiled as she gathered Puff in her arms and stood up from the bed.

Luke was leading them out when she felt something odd. He turned back frowning as time seemed to slow to a crawl and she felt herself being pulled backwards. Puff whined loudly in fear as she tipped back, yanked off her feet by burning hands. The last thing she saw before she was sucked back into darkness was the undeluded terror on Luke's face. And then. Nothing.

J.P. Hart

Chapter 22

Jessie was dangling in a tarnished steel cage with Puff clutched to her chest and her wings closed around them protectively. Outside the cage, creatures writhed and cackled at her, stabbing at her wings with spears as they swung helplessly above them. The smell of burning Sulphur threatened to make her choke as it scraped through her sinuses and down her throat. Puff shook in terror and whined.

Through the dark translucency of the energy that gave her wings form, she glared at Bernal. Dr. Jones stood to his left. And his God damned smug smile was right where it always was. Her fingers itched to claw it off his face. Her pendant burned against her skin, but the cage was preventing her from using it.

The one time she'd tried, the blast had ricocheted off the bars and hit them hard. She'd barely had the chance to shield Puff from the worst of it before it seared into her flesh, leaving her left arm numb. Bernal had laughed at her struggle and clapped like a delighted child.

He was so impressed by her power. She'd wanted to puke.

"I knew you were special," he said.

She grit her teeth as she tried to sooth Puff as best as she could with her right hand. "What do you want, Bernal?"

"I've told you before, my dear," he said with a sigh. "My friends call me Bernie."

"Lay off the drugs, Bernal," she said. "If you think we're friends, it's rotting your brain."

He tutted and shook his head. "You'll see things differently, soon," he said.

"Fat chance."

"How are the voices?" he asked and she ground her teeth. "Spirare and our voices," he chuckled. "Constantly hearing the balance at war can be quite maddening, can't it? The darkness whispers doubts and fear while the light coos and soothes, and all the while we are stuck in the middle playing devil's advocate for the truth."

"Your point?" she asked, but she really just wanted him to shut the fuck up.

"You need your bond-mate to keep your balance," he said. "Why do you think I made sure to cross your path with him as much as possible?"

"Because you get your jollies playing match maker?"

"Oh, no, my dear," he said. "His insistence that I bring you to MERCE was my first clue that I might finally have the key to controlling him. And, I needed to ensure that I could break Mr. Interitus when the time came."

"You kidnapped me because you wanted to break Luke?" she asked, narrowing her gaze at him.

"I kept him as my pupil after I retired from the ranks for a reason," he said. "The ruthless power I saw in him was extraordinary," he gloated. "I trained him. Molded him to be the perfect weapon. He was already so strongly in the grip of chaos, I knew it would be easy to sway him to our cause. But," he chuckled, "I needed to ensure a weakness to call him to heel if he got out of control. He had no family to exploit, no ties to this world. Until he found you," he said. His grin turned sadistic. "You have done your job quite nicely."

"Fuck you," she said with a hiss.

"Oh, so protective," he laughed. "Maybe I should have grabbed him instead, hmm? You *are* the most powerful Spirare I have come across," he said as he eyed her in appreciation. "But," he said as he held up a finger, "you're just a bit too tame. I need someone that I can break. And you are going to help me, my dear. That is, if I can convince you."

"Convince me of what?" she asked with a growl of irritation. "Get to the point."

"To join the cause," he said as he passed the creatures lining the walls of the crumbling room. As he reached the cage, he used his cane to turn it from below and she spun lazily to face the throne of twisted carcasses on a dais of bones. "The Legions are what all dark creatures are. Glorious chaos and unbound indulgence. Think of it. No rules, no constant battle between the darkness and the light. Just pure, unbridled passion set free. But, they need someone to lead them."

"And you want to be the biggest bastard of them all, right?" she asked as her eyes narrowed at the macabre chair. She remembered that throne from her nightmares. The fear had come from losing Daniel. But, the power had been seductive.

"Of course, my dear," he said with a chuckle. "Unfortunately, I don't have the strength to wield the artifact anymore. Eons of being torn down and rebuilt took too much of a toll on these old bones. But, who needs to hold the power, when one can simply control it?"

"Pass," she said with a bored expression making him frown.

"Excuse me?" he asked.

"Being the mascot for evil isn't exactly my idea of fun," she told him. "Besides, this place smells like shit."

"I see your usual wit has not left you," he said like he had a bad taste in his mouth. "We'll see how witty you are after a few centuries."

She laughed mirthlessly. "You really think it's going to take that long for Luke to find me? And he's not going to just give up and roll over to save me. He'll fight. He'd die before he'd join you. He's with three angels, two other Spirare, and a pissed off Brit with a fetish for fire. He'll be here before you can say 'my dear' one more time."

"I'm counting on it," he said with a smirk as he started to walk away. "You know, I was once a captive here, too, before I learned how much nicer the darkness is. That cage of forged darkness you're hanging in was my home once, too." He paused and looked back at her. "And, you know what the worst part of my whole ordeal was?"

"Do I look like I give a shit?" she asked.

"It was the idleness," he said as if she hadn't spoken and looked at the cage in appreciation. "Survivors fight, or flee," he shrugged. "Only the dead lay down. My. Dear."

Jessie grit her teeth and slid with her back to the bars as he chuckled all the way out of the room with Dr. Jones trailing behind him. She fought the urge to scream in frustration. She was trapped and helpless. The voices were already making her head throb as her distress added fuel to the fire. She needed Luke to regain her balance, but she prayed he stayed away. She needed to keep her boys safe. She needed to find a way to get them free on her own.

"Mommy?" Puff asked quietly.

"What, honey?" she asked back as she scratched the fur of his neck and rested her head on his.

"Don't worry," he whispered. "I'll protect you."

"I know you will, sweetheart," she said and hugged him tighter. "I know you will."

Chapter 23

Weeks passed into months and then into years. She'd been wearing the same jeans and oversized hoodie for five decades of idle Hell as Puff grew steadily in her arms. She'd fought and snapped every time Dr. Jones had brought them food in an effort to break free. Until he'd let them starve. When Puff had laid down and started to wheeze from hunger, she'd backed off.

Even then, he'd barely given them enough rotted scraps to feed one of them. She'd long since starved past the point that a human would have died and her bones felt brittle in her drying skin. Puff comforted her as best as he could when Bernal wasn't there to taunt and torture her, getting in her head and twisting her perception of reality into her worst nightmares in an effort to break her, but weakness as making it hard to reassure him that everything would work out for the best.

"Mom?" he asked when her eyes had drifted shut for too long. The high, clear sound of the child he'd been had started to deepen into that of a teen. His black fur had started to develop tinges of red over his joints and the tips of his ears as he'd gotten older, reminding her of how long it had been. "Mom, are you ok?" he asked as he put his head in her lap and whined in concern.

His broad head was almost the size of her torso by then and his ruby eyes turned sad as he looked at her.

"I'm fine, sweetheart," she said with a croak as a tear slid down her cheek.

We'renotfineWe'renotfineWe'renotfine

Just hold on. It'll be alright.

We'redoneWe'redoneWe'redone

They'll come for us.

Theyhavetostayaway

We'll get out of here.

"How are we doing today, my dear?" Bernal asked as he came for his daily visit.

"Better until you showed up," she said as Puff started to growl threateningly at him. It wouldn't do any good. He'd tried biting the bars and clawing at them. He'd even tried melting them with the fire he'd learned to belch on command but they hadn't budged. "The answer is still fuck off and die."

"I do grow tired of your rudeness, my dear," he said with a shake of his head.

"Well, I do grow tired of your face, Bernal," she said. She wanted to sound strong and show him that he couldn't break her, but she was too exhausted.

"How about you, child?" he asked Puff.

"You heard her," he said with a growl. "Fuck off and die."

She smiled weakly at him as he lifted his head and snarled. He was so strong. So much stronger than she was. He'd grown so much, but his life had been in a cage. Pride and regret swelled in her chest as tears started to roll down her cheeks. She'd done that to him. She'd failed to protect her son. Again.

"Why us, Bernal?" she asked quietly as she heard his cane clicking away from them against the stone floor. "That's the one thing I haven't been able to figure out."

"Fate, perhaps?" he said as he click-click-clicked toward them.

"They say the Primal Source has no conscious thought, but I'd like to believe it does. It didn't like the angels meddling in its plans by creating the Veil, so it brought you to me to help tear it down."

"You need someone to wield it for you," she said quietly. "But, it doesn't have to be Luke. You can't do it because you're not strong enough anymore after what they did to you. But, it doesn't have to be him. Just someone who will enjoy watching the world burn with you."

"Mom?" Puff whined at her. He could hear the resignation creeping into her voice.

"That is correct," Bernal said and she closed her eyes.

She looked into Puff's scared ruby eyes and breathed deep. They'd only seen the Purgatory they dangled helplessly in because she was either too weak or too stupid to save them. Could he remember what the sun looked like? Could he remember the cool wind on his face as he watched her and his father and his Grandpa play their games? She'd have resigned herself to an eternity there and happily served her sentence for her crimes had it not been for her son and the man she loved. They deserved more than that. They deserved to be free.

She closed her eyes and sent one last prayer to Luke that he could forgive her for her weakness and find the strength to move on. She breathed deep as she remembered his touch and his pride. The last thing she brought to the forefront of her mind was his rare, wide smile as he held Puff as a puppy in his arms the day they'd been taken so long ago. Her family.

"Mom?" Puff asked again as he shifted up onto his feet as best as the cage would allow and rubbed his big, flat head against her cheek to dry it. "Don't cry. It'll be ok."

"I know it will, sweetheart," she told him as she let the happiness she'd once known go. "I'll do it, Bernie. Promise me that you'll leave Luke alone and let my son go free. You don't need them. I'll wield the artifact for your cause," she said as she turned her head to look at him below her.

"So glad you are finally ready to see things my way, my dear," he said. "Deal."

Chapter 24

Jessie tumbled to the hard stone floor with Puff beside her as the bottom of the cage dropped out from beneath them the instant his agreement left his lips. She shook as she tried to stand, but her muscles weren't there to help her. She was little more than a skeleton in baggy jeans and an even baggier sweatshirt. She was broken.

Puff's head appeared under her as she tried again to push herself from the ground and he lifted her to her feet, panting from the effort. She leaned against him with her arm draped over his broad shoulders. She hadn't seen him stand to his full height since the cramped space of the cage had forced him onto his stomach. He was as big as horse.

"Mom, I don't understand," he said as he looked down at her. "Why are you giving up? Dad will be here soon."

"You're going to have to keep him away from me, sweetheart," she said. She couldn't risk him being captured. Once she gave herself over to the darkness, she wouldn't have anything of herself left for him to try and save. "Once you're safe, I need you to stay away, too."

"No," he whined. "It's my job to protect you."

"I know, honey," she said quietly. "And the best way you can do that is to keep yourself and your father safe."

He whined quietly as he looked at her. She didn't know what

was going through his head, but in the end he took a shaking breath and nuzzled her cheek. "I love you, Mom."

"I know you do, baby," she said and buried her face in his downy fur one last time. "I love you, too."

"I am so pleased with you, my dear," Bernal said as he came smiling up to where they stood. The creatures that made up their perpetual audience snarled and snapped in excitement as he approached. "You have done so well."

"Can it, Bernie," she said tiredly. "Let's just get this over with so my son can go home."

"Very well," he said with a smile and looked at Puff. "The artifact, if you don't mind," he said and held out his hand.

Puff whined once and looked at her. She nodded and he started to retch. He gagged hard and shook as he dropped his head low and started to cough violently. Flames licked at the sides of his muzzle as he moved his tongue, working the artifact out of his stomach. She coaxed and rubbed his shoulder until, with a hard, wet plunk, the stone dropped onto the floor covered in molten gastric juices.

He dropped to the ground once it was out and cringed as Jessie knelt beside him.

"I'm ok, Mom," he said weakly. "My stomach just hurts, that's all."

"You're so brave," she said and smoothed his fur. He was almost free. He'd do so well without her, she just had to make sure he could get out safe. "My brave little boy."

Bernal poked the flaming ball of puke with his cane until it started to cool and then slid it over to Jessie. "If you don't mind, my dear," he said.

"You never did like getting your hands dirty, did you?" she asked as she leaned to pick up the unassuming chunk of black and white marble the size of her palm.

"Not if I could help it," he said with a shrug as she wiped it off on her pants, scorching the dirty denim.

Energy surged through her as she held the artifact, filling out her hollow bones. It was still searing hot, burning into her flesh, but she relished the pain. It was the first real thing she'd felt in a long time. She breathed hard as she felt it pulling her back from the brink.

Her instincts whispered through her sweetly, soothing her, telling her to trust them. She surrendered to them as she felt herself begin to shake in fear. She lifted the artifact and cradled it to her chest. Warmth wrapped around her as her pendant started to burn against her skin, melting into her flesh with an agony so brilliant it bordered on ecstasy.

Images of her life flickered in her mind as she recalled the hatred that had formed her. Whispered fear and angry taunts hardened her against the world and their rules of conformity. Their distain had been her fuel. Their fear had been her fire. Bernal's quest for power had fanned it all.

She let the chaos of the world around her rip through her soul and scatter it to ashes on the wind. She was a hollow shell of solidified rage. And then the injustice of everything peaked at the crescendo of what had been done to her children. The artifact dissolved in her hands, absorbing into her skin as an image of Daniel flashed through her mind.

His messy, dark hair was shining in the sun as he ran and squealed happily through the dry grass of the park she'd taken him to. She'd chased him, and he'd laughed as he tried to get away. He'd held the artifact, too, she realized, and she saw that day through his eyes.

He'd been hiding while they played, beneath a tree that was gnarled and twisted with age. He'd seen a flash of light near him. A wavering in the air like a desert mirage.

He'd gone towards it, curious to see what it was. He'd found the rock in the dusty earth and picked it up. He'd been so excited to show it to her. He'd known it was special. But, it'd started to crumble in his hands. It'd soaked through his skin and into his heart where it ached, but he wasn't afraid. It'd told him not to be. He was a brave boy and it needed him to keep it safe. Safe from the bad man. He'd looked back at the wavering air and seen a face peering out at him.

It had been Bernal, furious that he'd been too late. Daniel had run from him. Run straight back and into Jessie's waiting arms. She was his everything. His whole world and the rock whispered to him that he needed to protect her. Like she protected him. They were sitting on the park bench when he'd asked her for a snow cone from the stand nearby. She'd smiled indulgently as she made him promise to stay put and he'd agreed. He'd needed to keep her safe.

He'd seen the bad man talking to the man in the leather vest and had known what would happen. The rock had told him to be brave. He'd slipped from the bench when Jessie's back was turned and ran into the tall grass to wait. The rock had covered him in dull light so she wouldn't know where he was. He'd heard Jessie's panicked voice as she'd screamed for him, but he'd bit his lip and stayed away.

The man in the leather vest had found him and took him to the barn. They'd ripped out his pockets while he cried, telling him to give back what he stole from the bad man. They didn't understand what they were looking for. All they could think about was the money the bad man had offered them. When they didn't find anything, they were told he'd swallowed it and to starve him until he gave it back. They'd hated themselves for it, but they'd done what he'd asked.

Daniel didn't let it go. His belly had hurt from being empty for so long and he'd whimpered in the dark when one of the men told him it would be ok. The man had been kind to him and tried to give him food, but his boss had threatened to kill him if he did it again.

"He's just a child," the kind man had said.

"He's a 2 mil payday," he boss had said.

"I can't," the kind man had said and walked away.

Daniel had watched as the kind man left and his boss followed him out. He'd heard a crack like thunder outside and the kind man didn't come back. His boss had, and he'd been so angry, he'd kicked Daniel hard.

"That was my brother," he'd screamed at Daniel. "You made me kill my brother!" The boss hadn't meant to do it. The bad man had wanted him alive to make Jessie cooperate. He'd needed her for his plan. She was special and he'd needed Daniel to make her behave. But, Daniel's belly didn't hurt anymore.

His soul had watched from the Void as Bernal had come to collect his prize, only to find the boy dead with nothing to show for it. He'd been so angry he'd set the little boy's body on fire to burn out the stone. But, Daniel had been smart. He had taken the stone with him into the Void to keep it safe. But, he couldn't leave yet. He had to make sure he kept his Mommy safe, too. But, he was just a little boy without a body.

The rock had whispered that it could help and Daniel had smiled when part of him pulled away to make a small black ball of fur with bright red eyes. The rock went into the puppy. Daniel told him to run and find Jessie. She was the best Mommy in the world and she would keep them safe. He gave the puppy all of the memories he'd had of his time with her and made the puppy promise to grow up big and strong to keep her safe.

As the puppy panted happily and trotted away to find his Mommy, Daniel smiled and turned away to go home.

Jessie staggered under the weight of the memories as the artifact whispered through her mind. It had needed her to see the balance in everything, to understand that no one thing is right or wrong. She was the one who could hold it and be safe. She was the one who would end existence to save innocence. Her life was balance. She was love in harmony with pain.

Energy cascaded in a waterfall of pale light as she lifted her arms to the sides and accepted her fate. Puff stood beside her and lifted his head to it with a howl as he basked in the power. Bernal cringed away as the creatures started to stomp and cry out in preparation for their release.

Her wings exploded from her back and solidified into black, pearlescent feathers. She beat them once to hover as the energy around them began to fade. She and Puff steamed with the remains and she looked at Bernal in placid question.

"My beautiful avenging angel," he breathed in awe. "Will you burn with me?"

She smiled peacefully as she looked down at him, feeling out the consciousness of the Legions around her and taking control as she had with the monster in the meadow so many decades before. Silence fell amongst the Legions in the stronghold that stretched the expanse of the Void as she made her intentions known. They would finally be free of their prison forever. But, they could not have the worlds.

"Nope," she said with a smirk. She shot him the finger and rolled her shoulders forward to swing her hands together.

Chapter 25

Jessie stepped out of the Veil with Puff at her side into the blistering wind of an early season storm. It had taken them a couple of years of wandering through the ashes leftover from destroying the Legions, but it had been easy to keep moving once they were free. She'd wanted to scour the wasteland of the Void to make sure nothing had survived, but Puff had told her it would have taken centuries to search the entire plane of the Void's existence.

He would know, she thought. He'd told her of his journey to find her while they walked through the ash, only stopping to hunt for food and rest, and had explained that the way his kind aged, he only got a year older for every five that he lived. He'd spent most of his childhood hopping through from one side of the Veil to the other to stay one step ahead of the Legions and Bernal. Though he'd never paused in the Void for long because the danger had been too great, he'd lived twenty-odd years before he'd found her. His search for her had taken him from infancy to adolescence but he said he'd do it again if it meant that he could have his family.

When they would stop to rest on their journey back, she would feel the constant echoes of Luke terror and rage pulsing through the Veil to her heart, frozen in time at the moment when they'd disappeared. That was her beacon to get home. If they hadn't left when they did, he would have brought the Veil down just to find them. He would have stopped at nothing to get his family back where is belonged.

She curled her wing up to shield her face against the icy blast of wind and looked out to the cabin a few yards away. She couldn't see where she'd stepped with her father anymore, but she could feel the fresh trail of his energy as he'd led her to the door. She squinted at Puff and patted his shoulder to make sure he was ok. He licked her cheek and put his head down against the wind. With a shake of her head, she glared in the direction of the storm and the force stopped dead.

"Fucking wind," she said as she shivered.

"My mom," Puff said with a chuckle. "The badass."

"What? It's cold," she said and pushed on his shoulder. He laughed and pushed her back with his head on her arm. "Come on, kid. Let's get inside before your dad pops an aneurism."

"You know, there's something I've been meaning to ask you. It's been bothering me for a while, but I just," he let the sentence hang and she patted his shoulder in encouragement. "How did you know that would work?" he asked as they trekked towards the cabin. "The whole bang, boom, dead Legions thing. When you told Bernal you were giving up, how did you know?"

"True facts?" she asked as she looked up at him from the corner of her eye.

"True facts," he said with a nod.

"I didn't," she said and he looked at her in surprise and stopped. "I really had given up. It would have killed me to be without you and your father, but if it meant you'd be safe, I was willing to give in and lay down."

"I don't ever want you to do that again," he said and rubbed his head against her arm. "Not for me or anybody. I don't think that kind of sacrifice is worth it."

"You don't realize how much you mean to me," she said as she started to choke up a little. She'd thought the same thing when she'd seen what Daniel had done for her.

"But still," he said with a whine.

"We can argue what is worth it until the cows come home, kiddo," she said with a shrug. "But sometimes, it's necessary to make the painful, terrifying choice to protect the ones you love. That's the nature of true balance, and the world needs that balance between darkness and light to continue to exist."

"Won't the Legions being dead throw the whole universal balance thing off, though?" he asked as they started walking again. "I mean, if there's no more evil in the world, doesn't that mean there's too much good?"

"Not really," she said with a shrug as she huddled into Luke's hoodie. It was torn and burned in places, and it stunk to high Hell, but it was still warm. "They represented chaos incarnate. But life outside of the Void isn't all sunshine and rainbows, kid. A friend once told me that even though there's darkness and light, evil is just a matter of prospective."

"Sounds like a smart guy," he said.

"Yeah," she chuckled. "You'll like him. He's tattooed to his eyeballs and has a face full of steel."

"You think they'll remember us?" Puff asked with a whine as they reached the top of the crest that would lead them down to the cabin's front porch.

"Honey, to them, we've only been gone for about thirty seconds, forty-five tops. Dollars to doughnuts, if we wait here any longer, your dad's going to come tearing out of that door like the devil's on his heels snorting fire and looking for something to slaughter," she said.

"What's a doughnut?" he asked and she chuckled.

"Something I'm going to have to introduce you to as soon as we get home," she said and then frowned as she looked at him.

"What?" he asked and turned his head to look at his back. "Do I have something in my fur?"

"No," she said and shook her head. "I'm just thinking about how difficult it's going to be to get you into the elevator at MERCE. I think we're going to have to move."

"Awe man," he whined and started to pout. "I liked it there. It was pretty and I liked the stars."

"We'll figure something out," she assured him and patted his shoulder affectionately.

Ahead of them the front door burst open on a roar of rage. Luke's big body filled the doorframe, puffing like an angry bull, and his eyes snapped ruby fire. He was barking orders as he marched at double time into the snow with his sword drawn.

"Told you," she said with a chuckle to Puff.

"Dad!" he howled and Luke pulled up short. He stared as Puff barreled down the incline towards him. His swords slipped from his hand and clattered to the ground. Puff caught Luke in the chest with his head and knocked him to the ground, licking his face ruthlessly and wagging his big bushy tail.

Luke's face was a comical mash of confusion and shock as she sauntered over to them, shaking her head.

"Dad, Dad, I missed you so much," Puff said as he continued to lick Luke's face and nuzzle him. When he was satisfied that his father was suitably bathed in slobber, he hopped back and started dancing on his front paws like he had when he was a puppy. "Dad, oh my god, you're not going to believe how amazing Mom was. I mean holy shit, Dad, it was awesome. There's so much to tell you."

"I told you he really does love you," she said as Luke jumped to his feet and stared at her. He put his hands on her face and shoulders like he wasn't sure she was real, breathing heavily. His ruby eyes started to swim as his relief at finding her mixed with her relief of being found.

"How?" he breathed.

"Long story," she said with a shrug. He tackled her in a hug so tight she knew he was afraid of letting go and popped her off her feet as he stood. She wrapped her arms around his neck and held on just as tightly. "Easy big guy," she soothed and kissed his cheek. He was shaking. "It's ok, now. We're safe."

"I thought I'd lost you," he whispered painfully and she pushed as much calming reassurance into him as she could.

"You did," she said and he looked at her in fear. "But, we found our way back," she whispered to him and he buried his face in her neck again. "We always will."

He kissed her so deeply and completely she thought she would burst as their tangling emotions rocked through her soul.

"Ew," Puff complained and dropped to his belly to roll in the snow with a hacking cough. She reluctantly broke away from Luke to look at her son. "I think I'm dying from lovey-dovey overload," he said in his most pathetic voice.

"Asshole," she said and wiggled free from Luke to throw a snowball at him as he laughed. He got up and started hopping from side to side as she continued to pelt him with snowballs.

"Get a room," he said and used his tail to sweep snow at her in retaliation.

"We have one," she smiled at him. "And you're not allowed in it for at least a week when we get home."

He gagged and sneezed at her.

After Luke finished gawking at the size his son had gotten to be, they went inside and filled everyone in on what had happened in the Void. Luke looked like he wanted to resurrect Bernal just to kill him all over again. Her dad just stared at her in amazement. The angels looked at her like she was the messiah. And, Chantel giggled gleefully when Puff recounted her destruction of the Legion in all its gory detail.

"Dude," Kristoff said to Luke. "Wife her."

"Yeah, Luce," Gabby agreed. "Wife her hard. Or I will."

"I told you, Gabby," Jessie said as she curled into Luke's side on the couch and wrapped her arm around his chest. "I appreciate the offer, but I'm pretty sure his sword is bigger."

Luke had finally chuckled at that and shifted her so she was sitting across his lap with her head in the crook of his neck. She breathed him in and relaxed as his hand found hers and their fingers laced together. "Te iubesc, draga mea," he whispered to her.

"English, fucker," she said and he chuckled.

"I love you, sweetheart," he said.

"Oh," she smiled and waited for him to look at her. "I love you, too."

When they returned to MERCE shortly afterwards, Zadkiel offered to take Chantel in Kristoff's Jeep to let her and Luke get home together.

"He's a good man," he'd whispered in her ear when she'd given him a hug goodbye. "Take care of him."

"Did you hit your head?" she asked with a chuckle.

"I saw his reaction to losing you," he said seriously. "If you hadn't come back when you did, I doubt there would have been a world left when he was done. He's still an asshole," he smirked, "but, that's the kind of beast I want at your side."

She'd shaken her head and joined Luke where he was waiting with Puff a few feet away to step through the Veil. They'd come out again on the balcony of their apartment and Puff had opted to stay outside for the night.

"I like the fresh air," he told her when she'd asked him why. She understood. He'd spent his life either running from danger or in a cage. She kissed his muzzle and went inside to let her son breathe in peace for the first time.

Luke closed the door to their room and secured the curtain as she stripped out of her jeans and his hoodie. She examined them and frowned. With a hard exhale, she tossed them in the corner of the room. She'd have to take them to the trash in the morning. Or let Puff burn them. Either way, there was no salvaging them.

"What's the matter, inimioara?" Luke asked as she pulled the ties out of her hair and shook out the length as best she could. Her hair wasn't as brittle as it had been before the Primal Source has restored her health, but it was still enough of a pain to make her consider cutting it all off.

"I liked that hoodie," she said as he came over to her and put his hands on her waist. "I'll have to buy you a new one."

"I'm not worried about it," he said as he tucked a strand of her hair behind her ear. "Clothing is replaceable. You're not. I'm just glad you're safe."

She exhaled slowly and rested her head between his pecs, listening to the sound of his heart. She thought of how hopeless she'd been in the Legions' stronghold, how sure she'd been that she would never see him again. She wrapped her arms around his waist and held him tightly. He slid his hand into her hair and pressed his lips to the top of her head.

"I'm not going anywhere," he promised her quietly as he brushed her mind and heart through his touch. "Now," he said gruffly as he tried to get his own emotions under control, "go shower. You smell funny."

"Yeah," she said with a chuckle and looked up at him, "Well, your face is annoying."

He gave her a crooked smile and winked at her before releasing her with a swat to the behind. She shuffled into the shower and scrubbed her skin until she thought it would bleed to get the last fifty years off. She was almost finished when he joined her and started kissing her neck. She chuckled and shook her head. She wanted to be with him again. To her, they hadn't been together in half a century and she missed his touch.

When he reached her throat and moved her pendant aside, he paused. "What?" she asked. "I wasn't done with you yet."

He touched the skin he was looking at and pushed the image of what he saw into her mind. The flesh was scarred in the shape of her pendant just above her cleavage. Beneath his finger, the raw energy of the Primal Source fragment pulsed, making them both groan from the surge. "It's still with you," he said breathlessly.

She smiled as she reached for the clasp of her necklace and took her pendant off. She turned in his arms and closed the chain around his neck instead. He breathed deeply as it settled against his skin below the hollow of his throat. "Never take it off," she said, repeating his instructions to her.

He caught her palm as she moved to release him and kissed her palm. "Got it," he said with a smile and pressed her hand to his cheek. He finished rinsing them off and carried her to bed. He settled her in first under the blankets before sliding in next to her and gathering her in his arms.

He felt her exhaustion mingling with her desire to be with him again and chuckled. "Not tonight, mândra mea," he said ruefully and she sighed. He was quiet for a while as he held her and she could feel something bothering him.

"What's wrong?" she asked with a yawn.

"I was just thinking."

"About?" she prompted him. She didn't have to ask, but she wanted to hear his voice.

"The worst part about everything that happened, besides not getting to shred Bernal for what he did to you two," he said, "is that I missed so much of Puff's life. I mean, he was just a baby when you were taken. And now," he sighed. "I didn't get to watch him grow up."

"You still have time," she reminded him, thinking of what Puff had explained about a hellhound's lifespan. "Believe me. You're his dad. He loves you. That's all that really matters."

"I know," he said quietly, but it was still eating at him.

"You know what else?" she asked and sat up to look down at him with a smirk.

"What?"

"We can always have another one," she teased.

"I don't think we have enough room for another hellhound in the family," he said with a smirk and she smacked his arm. "I know what you mean," he said. "And, I think I like that idea. But I get to name them."

"Them?" she asked with an eyebrow raised.

"I like having a big family," he smiled. "You know, just seven or eight. Maybe nine. Hey, we could name them after the Fellowship of the Ring."

She smacked him with a pillow. When he started listing the characters by name, she continued to pummel him much to his amusement. When he was done, she kissed him until he changed his mind on the "not tonight" decision.

"You want to start trying now?" she asked with a chuckle.

"Maybe not try," he said with a shrug as he rolled her onto her back and kissed her neck. "But, at least practice."

"Practice does make perfect," she said and gasped as he found what he was looking for.

That was her life, she thought later as they laid quietly in the dark with Luke snoring softly above her head. An angel for a father. A hellhound for a son. Her devil in her arms. And, for the first time, real hope for the future.

If you enjoyed MERCE,

Turn the page for a Sneak Peek of Book 2…

Spirare

Chapter 1

Jessie perched on the edge of the rooftop of the Republic Plaza in downtown Denver with her eyes locked on Tremont Place fifty-six stories below. The frigid wind blasted her face and hands where they were left exposed by her scarf and brown leather bomber jacket, leaving her skin cracked and numb. She shifted her black pearl, feathered wings as another sharp gust threated to push her over. The tiny black speaker in her right ear thrummed to the beat of "Dragula" over the open com she shared with the three other Spirare on her team that night.

Keeping her hands on the icy cement border ringing the roof, she edged her 6" heeled boot to the side and slid her center of gravity over, watching her prey below. Though the moon wasn't quite full yet, the ambient light of the yellowed streetlamps gave his skin a ghostly tone. The man had ice white hair and was as pale as a stick of chalk, making him easy to spot on the nearly deserted street. In her ear, the music faded and a slightly accented rumble overpowered the song.

"Eyes up, focul iadului," her Seraph said.

She rolled her mismatched eyes and touched the mic strapped to her throat to open the line. "I got him."

"Do not engage, Jessica," he reminded her for the millionth time since they'd picked up the Energy Vampire's trail earlier that night. "Let me take him down."

"Yeah yeah," she said with a grumble and shifted her body again as the E.V. reached the corner. "Moving position," she told the team. "You got me, Mitch?"

"I got you," the Arch Spirare confirmed in a deep tenor that sounded like a squeak compared to their lead's growly bass.

She leapt into a glide to land on the Cache Bank and Trust Building across the street. It was lower, but she was still out of the E.V.'s sensory range. "He's on 17th," she said. If he kept going, he'd reach Glenarm Place and circle back towards the bars and restaurants that had yet to clear out. He'd already made the circuit twice. She looked at the digital readout on her watch. Last call. Son of a bitch was hunting for drunks. They had to take him down before he found his next meal. "I'm going to get his attention."

"Jessie," her Seraph growled in her ear in warning.

"Just a little nudge," she said. "We need to get him away from the Mundanes if you're going to take him down and we're running out of time."

Luke cursed in Romanian before letting go of his mic, allowing another deep voiced chuckle break through. "Your wife's pretty ballsy, boss," the other Arch Spirare said.

"I'm not his wife, Oscar," she said. Again.

"Never will be if she gets herself killed," Luke added.

Jessie ignored the jibe and dropped like a stone, using her wings to buffer her decent into the small alleyway between the Bank and Trust building and the red brick building beside it. At the pace the E.V. was walking, she had about thirty seconds before he passed the opening to the small space. She recalled her wings to dissolve back into the ether and sat down on the ground.

"Get ready," she told Luke and the others.

"Coming up behind you, chīsai," Mitch said, using the Japanese word for tiny to refer to Jessie.

"Baiting the trap," Jessie said and opened her soul to draw power from the Primal Source through the scar on her chest just as the E.V. came into view twenty feet away.

The E.V.'s mirrored gaze snapped to her, freezing him mid stride as he lifted his head to scent the air like the predator he was. She tilted her head and smiled sweetly at him as he started towards her warily. Behind her, she felt the shadows move against her back and she watched the darkness ripple against the wall from the corner of her eye. Mitch was using his Spirare mark to conceal himself.

The E.V. came closer with his eyes going wider in greed. He could feel Mitch's energy mixing with hers, but he couldn't see him. It was like putting a bottomless supply of heroin in front of an addict and crooking your finger to beckon them closer. She leaned back on her hands and stretched her feet out in front of her with her ankles slightly apart. She flipped her waist length, black braid over her shoulder carelessly and gave him her best come hither stare. He moved closer and a knowing smirk spread across his thin lips.

She brushed his mind with her own and caught the edge of some very XXX rated ideas involving her and where he was going to sink his fangs. She whispered encouragement into his thoughts to draw him in. He tilted his head back and breathed deeply. He leveled his eyes on Jessie with a grin that bordered on manic and between one heartbeat and the next, he was on her.

ABOUT THE AUTHOR

I don't like talking about myself, so I'll keep it short and sweet. I'm almost 30 years old with an overactive imagination, a passion for escaping into a good fantasy novel every now and then, and I'm tired of working for other people. I've been writing since I was a kid, but decided to actually put something to print when my family gave me the swift kick in the ass I needed to get it done.

I love my gamer friends and family, and I thought of them when I wrote this. I got my feet wet in the fantasy world with D&D, VtM, and online (chat based) RPG. I admire and adore cosplayers and LARPers, they are some of the coolest people I know, and I wanted to do something for them as much as myself.

And, thus, MERCE was born.

I hope you enjoy.

– J.P. Hart

www.ingramcontent.com/pod-product-compliance
Lightning Source LLC
Chambersburg PA
CBHW030918120626
46554CB00001B/202